ROBERT
SWINDELLS

HYDRA

Illustrated by Mark Robertson

CORGI YEARLING BOOKS

HYDRA
A CORGI YEARLING BOOK : 0 440 86313 9

First published in Great Britain by Doubleday,
a division of Transworld Publishers

PRINTING HISTORY
Doubleday edition published 1991
Corgi Yearling edition published 1993
Reissued 1999

11 13 15 17 19 20 18 16 14 12

Corgi Yearling Books are published by Transworld Publishers,
61–63 Uxbridge Road, London W5 5SA,
a division of The Random House Group Ltd,
in Australia by Random House Australia (Pty) Ltd,
20 Alfred Street, Milsons Point, Sydney, NSW 2061, Australia,
in New Zealand by Random House New Zealand Ltd,
18 Poland Road, Glenfield, Auckland 10, New Zealand
and in South Africa by Random House (Pty) Ltd,
Endulini, 5a Jubilee Road, Parktown 2193, South Africa.

Printed and bound in Great Britain by
CPI Antony Rowe, Eastbourne

For Heather

Special thanks to Jill, Monica and Timothy, my West Country advisers!

Hȳ´dra *n.* (Gk Myth.) Many-headed monster of marshes of Lerna, whose heads grew again as they were cut off, killed by Hercules.

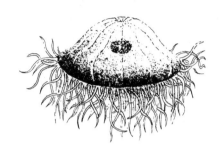

O N E

It was sick and hungry and a long, long way from home. It had little brain but it sensed that the tank was a hostile environment and it cruised around the wall, revolving slowly about its axis, bumping the frost-rimed metal till it found the door. As the floater's soft bulk bumped against it, the door moved.

The floater felt the motion and bumped again. Minute ice-flakes, dislodged from the hinges, drifted down, melting in the first waft of warm air as the door swung outward.

The temperature inside the tank rose a half-degree. The floaters, half-poisoned by the chemical cocktail mist on which they fed, didn't notice. As the creature entered the airlock, the woman jabbed the CLOSE button and the door swung slowly, clunking into its housing. Smiling behind her face-mask, she opened the outer door and stood aside.

The floater moved out into the barn. Eyeless, it felt the faint pull of starlight and followed, passing through the great open doorway and drifting away in the dark.

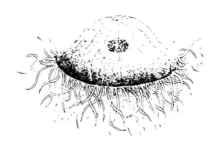

T W O

Ben knew exactly where his enemy would be waiting and there was nothing he could do about it. School was only a minute's walk from the front door but you had to pass the churchyard and that's where Barry would be. He always was. You could set off early – quarter past eight even – and he'd be there. Or you could wait till seconds before the bell then run, and he'd come loping out, throwing his arms round you from behind and trailing his feet till his weight stopped you. They got up early at Cansfield Farm and Barry didn't mind waiting. He didn't mind being late either, so you couldn't win.

Once or twice, Ben had crossed the High Street and pelted by on the other side, hoping the traffic would hold the bully up till he could reach the schoolyard. It had worked too, but it wasn't worth it. It made Barry mad and he came after Ben at breaktime, chasing him into a corner and banging his head on the wall, hissing, 'Thought you'd fool me, did you? Thought you'd make a prat out of old Barry, eh?' For some reason he only picked on Ben once a day, so Ben usually walked into the morning ambush to get it over with.

It wasn't his favourite solution though. His favourite solution would be to spin round as Barry came at him and punch him right between the eyes, then a karate-kick to the side of the head and stamp on his fingers as he lay on the pavement. It was a daydream of Ben's that he'd do it one day with Midge Fixby watching, but he knew he wouldn't. He was no fighter.

Ben always got a funny feeling when he thought about Midge, and he thought about her a lot. They were in the same class, and Ben was spending a lot of time lately gazing across at her when he should be doing other things. He couldn't help it, and he couldn't understand why she had this effect on him. Midge had blonde hair and blue eyes but she wasn't what you'd call pretty, and most of the kids thought her weird. She didn't join in much and was often to be seen standing alone in a corner of the schoolyard, gazing into space. If you asked her what she was doing she'd say 'thinking', but if you asked her what about, she'd say, 'oh, nothing', and walk away. And she was so thin. Really thin. She seemed to concentrate on balancing her head on the slender stem of her neck as she teetered off on her spindly legs.

The churchyard gates were coming up. Ben braced himself. Two seconds and Barry would be on him. One second. Now.

Nothing happened. He glanced left at the pink gravel pathway and crowded mossy headstones and saw no coarse, mocking face, no big raw hands, no boots, size eight.

No Barry.

The relief was unbelievable. He was floating through sunlight and bird-song – looking forward to his day, to school. And this was how life might be if there were no Barry Cansfield.

Hey. He grinned, catching his lower lip between his teeth. Maybe there isn't. Maybe something got him. His father's bull, or some clanking farm contraption. Something really messy. Nothing to laugh at, of course. Rotten to laugh, but still—

Crossing the High Street, Ben Lockwood laughed out loud for the first time in weeks.

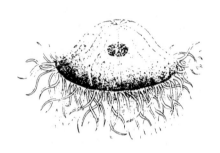

T H R E E

'Hey, Locky – come over here a minute.'

'What for?' Ben was suspicious. Wayne Daykin wasn't a friend and neither were the three lads with him. It would be a shame to dodge Barry and then get done over by somebody else.

'What d'you mean, what for? I've got something to tell you, bonehead.'

Ben went over to them. 'What?'

'You know Cansfield Farm?'

Something kicked in Ben's chest and he said, 'It's Barry, right? Something's happened to him.'

'Naw!' Daykin's eyes mocked. 'Don't you wish though, Locky, eh?'

'Don't we all,' said one of the other boys, and everybody laughed.

Daykin grinned and shook his head. 'What's happened is, they've found another of those circles.'

'Up Cansfield?'

'Yeah. Same place as before, practically. I seen it from the bus just now. There's cars and stuff and guys with cameras and binoculars and Dan Cansfield going ape-shape t'other side the hedge, trying to keep 'em all out.'

Ben grinned. 'Brandishing his gun, I bet.'

'Naw. Wouldn't dare. Not with the coppers watching.'

'Police're there?'

'Oh, aye. Looking for clues. You know – stickers with "Young Farmers do it in wellies" on 'em. They're sure it's that lot.'

Ben looked at him. 'D'you think it is Young Farmers?'

Daykin shook his head. 'My dad does, but I don't. I reckon it's alien spacecraft.'

'My mum says it's got something to do with the Army,' volunteered a freckly, red-headed boy. 'Some sort of secret weapon.'

'Who gives a toss what your mum says, Ginger?' sneered Daykin. 'It's alien spacecraft I tell you, on reconnaissance missions. They're sussing us out before launching an invasion. That's why they put all those daft explanations in the papers – helicopters and mice and people dancing round maypoles. It's to fool everyone so they won't panic.'

'I'd like to get a really close look at it,' said Ben.

Daykin laughed. 'No chance. You know what Dan Cansfield's like about trespassers. He'll shoot you as soon as look at you.'

'We could go at night.'

'Not this time of year we couldn't. Don't get dark till near midnight. Your folks let you stay out till then?'

Ben shook his head. 'No way.'

'Well, there y'are, then.'

The bell rang and the group broke up. Ben joined the crowd trooping into school, but with crop circles, alien invasions and Midge Fixby cramming his skull all day his work was less than brilliant. He got a smile from Midge in English though, and when he walked in the house at tea-time his mum was waiting with another mystery.

'Hi, Mum – what's for tea?'

' 'Lo, love. It's frozen pizzas, I'm afraid.'

'Aw, Mum.'

'I know, Ben, but it's Tuesday and I have to reopen the library at six.'

'It's Tuesday about five times a week if you ask me. Why can't somebody else open the rotten library?'

'Because there isn't anybody else, dear – not now that Mrs Dalby's retired. And it isn't a rotten library, it's a good one.'

Ben's mother ran the village library. It was small because Little Pitney was small, and it never opened mornings except Saturdays. It opened five afternoons and two evenings – Tuesdays and Thursdays. On

14

these two days Mum was in a bit of a rush and tea had to be something quick. It was OK when it was burgers or fish fingers, but frozen pizzas were dead boring, especially with baked potatoes and salad. Chips were Ben's favourite. He'd happily have eaten them every tea-time but his mother rationed him.

He hung his jacket on the bannister and returned to the kitchen. 'What time do we eat?'

His mother was defrosting a pizza in the microwave. She sighed. 'When your father gets in, of course. Honestly, Ben, you ask that question practically every day and the answer's always going to be the same.'

'Well, I'm starving. It's hungry work, learning.'

'I'm hungry too, dear, but I don't notice as much because I'm busy. Have you nothing to do?'

Ben shrugged. 'I could clean Michaelangelo out, I suppose. Feed him. Maybe he'll let me share his grub when he sees I'm dying.' Michaelangelo was a hamster. He lived in a fish-tank in the shed. Ben crossed the kitchen and went out, pinching a bit of lettuce from the cutting board as he passed.

The afternoon sun was warm but it was cool inside the shed. Cool and dim. It smelled of sawdust and creosote and Ben liked it. It was where he came when he wanted to be by himself. He was never quite alone because there was Michaelangelo, but hamsters aren't forever asking if you've brushed your teeth or tidied your room or washed behind your ears. Ben tapped on the fish-tank and Michaelangelo's nose came poking out of the ball of shavings in a corner. 'Come on, Mick – see what I've got for you.' He removed the tank's metal cover and dangled the shred of lettuce. The hamster peered short-sightedly, its pink nose working. 'Come on.' Ben twitched the lettuce and Michaelangelo came bustling over to sniff at it. 'I know,' sighed Ben. 'Boring, isn't it, but at least you don't have to wait for Dad, and you don't have to eat pizza with it either.'

The hamster began nibbling the lettuce, its busy jaws drawing in the shred with a tiny crunching sound. Ben let go his end and bent, sliding a bag of fresh sawdust from under the bench. He lifted Michaelangelo out of the tank and let the little creature explore the benchtop while he cleaned out its home. He'd topped up the water bottle and was filling Michaelangelo's dish with sunflower seeds when he heard his father's car.

'Hi, Dad.' His father was dropping cubes of butter in a tureen of cut beans as Ben went into the kitchen.

'Hello, Ben. How was school?'

'All right.' Ben wasn't the only one who asked the same question every day. How was school. What are you supposed to say?

They sat down and the meal began. Ben attacked his food, only half listening as his parents told each other about their boring day. Dad lectured at a college in Swindon. He nearly always had some story to tell about what so-and-so said to what's-his-face and what what's-his-face said in reply. It wasn't exactly sparkling stuff, and neither were Mum's contributions. Guess who came in the library today. Well – who? The Queen? Dracula? The entire Arsenal soccer team? No. Old Mrs somebody-or-other from t'other end of the High Street. Who cares, for Pete's sake? Ben made his beans into a pyramid and bulldozed it with his fork. Something his mother said caught his attention. Cansfield. He continued to toy with his beans, but he was listening too.

'—and there was that poor Frieda Cansfield, buying the *Daily Telegraph* and asking for tahini of all things. Tahini at Tarkington's – can you imagine?'

Dad chuckled, which meant he couldn't imagine. Ben looked up.

'What's tahini?'

'Sesame paste,' said his mother. 'It's used in cooking, but I wouldn't have thought that sort of cooking would go down well at Cansfield. More your beef and three veg with suet pudding to follow, I'd have said. And as for the *Telegraph*—'

Her husband shrugged and smiled. 'You never can tell, Emma – perhaps the Cansfields have changed. They may move in completely different circles these days for all we know.'

'Circles?' Ben nodded eagerly. 'There is a new one at Cansfield. Wayne Daykin saw—' He broke off as his parents chuckled. 'What's funny? What have I said?'

His mother reached out and ruffled his hair. 'Nothing, darling, it's all right. Your father didn't mean that sort of circle, that's all.'

Ben flushed. 'What sort then?'

'Well, what your dad meant was, perhaps the Cansfields have some new friends – the sort who cook with tahini and read the *Daily Telegraph*. D'you see?'

Ben nodded. 'But there *is* a new circle, Mum. It's in the wheatfield by the road.' He frowned. 'What sort of people would want to make friends with old Dan Cansfield anyway?'

'Ben.' His father shot him a disapproving glance. 'It's Mr Cansfield to you, not "old Dan". How would you feel if one of your friends referred to your mother as "old Emma Lockwood"?'

'I'd smack him right in the teeth, Dad.' Ah yes, but would I? he wondered.

'Well then, you must show a little respect for other people's parents, lad.'

'Yes, Dad. Sorry.' He wanted to talk about the circle but his parents didn't seem interested. They probably believed crop circles were a hoax, but he didn't. They were genuine enough, though Ben wasn't sure about Wayne Daykin's space invaders theory. Bit far-fetched, that. Maybe this circle had something to do with tahini and the *Telegraph*. Anyway, he knew what he was going to do. As soon as tea was over, he'd get his bike out and take a ride past Cansfield Farm. It was broad daylight and there'd be plenty of people about.

No danger there, surely?

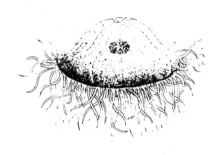

F O U R

'No use yelling at me, Wanda – it was you left the door unfastened.' Rex Exley, tall, thin and stooped, with pale crinkly hair, paced the barn floor, his shoes rapping on the boards. 'I never go near the revolting things, as you know.'

'Oh, I know all right.' Wanda Free was small, dark-haired, with glittering black eyes. 'There was certainly no sign of you when I was stumbling about in the middle of last night trying to put things right. Sound asleep, you were. Snoring like a pig.'

'I don't snore.' The man sounded indignant.

'No, and you don't do much of anything else either. I sometimes wonder why I brought you in on this in the first place.'

'Oh, that's easy.' The man smiled. 'Cash. I had it,

you needed it. And then of course there are my matchless journalistic skills, which will come into their own when you've finished doing whatever it is you do with those – things in there.' He gestured towards the great round tank which occupied more than half the space in the barn. It was four metres high and sixteen in diameter. The gleaming curve of its wall was punctuated here and there by small, round windows. Observation ports, the woman called them, though it was almost impossible to see in through the rime which fogged the thick glass.

'If we're going to be besieged by cops, reporters and assorted rubberneckers every five minutes, I'll never finish. Why don't you use some of those so-called journalistic skills to get rid of 'em, Rex?'

The man threw up his hands. 'I've tried, Wanda, but it gets more difficult each time. When we had that first escape I managed to plant the idea that the circle was made by people dancing in the corn or whatever they call it. The second time I said it was the wash from low-flying helicopters. Last time it was wood pigeons feeding. Not so good, I admit, but there's a limit even to my ingenuity. If these escapes continue and circles go on appearing, somebody's bound to get curious. Some tenacious amateur sleuth who won't be deflected by cock-and-bull stories is going to discover our secret and blow it wide open, and that'll be the end of the world exclusive, the book and most of the glory. I say let's go public now, before something like that happens.'

'No.' The woman's lips were a thin crimson slash. 'I told you before – I'm not handing the floaters over till I know everything there is to know about them. When those creatures belong to the world, I'm going to be the world's expert on them.'

The man shrugged. 'What's to know, Wanda? They're big, they're slow and they're stupid. We know that already. What else is there?'

'How they reproduce, for one thing.'

'Reproduce?'

'You know – breed. Where do baby floaters come from? How long does a floater live? Stuff like that.'

'You're becoming obsessed with the things, if you ask me.'

'I didn't ask you, Rex. You keep the busybodies away and leave the science to me, all right?'

'All right, Wanda. I'll do my best, but you be as quick as you can and remember what I said. That tenacious amateur sleuth could be approaching at this very moment.'

The woman looked at him. 'And if he is, you'll know exactly how to fix him, won't you?'

'Fix him?'

The woman lifted her chin and drew a rigid finger across her throat. 'Fix him,' she said.

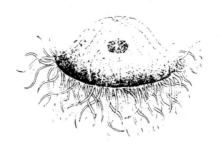

F I V E

Ben's mother looked at her watch. 'Quarter to six and I must fly. Be a pet and do the dishes, Ben.'

'I wish I was a pet,' muttered Ben, thinking of Michaelangelo. 'Pets just eat and leave the dishes to somebody else.' He said this softly, so that his father wouldn't hear. Aloud he said, 'Sure, Mum. No problem.' It had been a good day – why spoil it now?

It was ten past six when he rode his bike down the path and swung right along High Street. Cansfield Farm was half a mile away. He'd be there in a couple of minutes.

He'd just passed the pub – the Goose, its car park empty at this time of day – when he saw Midge Fixby standing at the bottom of Tansy Road. Something fluttered inside his chest. He pulled in, braking. 'Hi, Midge.'

'Oh, hello, Ben.'

'What you doing?'

'Nothing. Where you off to?'

'Cansfield Farm. I want to get a look at that circle. You coming?'

'Dunno.'

'Aw, come on, Midge.'

'Have to fetch my bike.'

'Go on then – I'll wait.'

You bet I'll wait, he thought, as the girl turned and ran, giraffe-like, up narrow Tansy Road. It had been a great day, and it wasn't over yet.

Cansfield land started where High Street became the Warminster Road. As they approached the farm, Ben and Midge saw a line of vehicles parked along one side of the road, and a line of red and white cones along the other. People – twenty or thirty of them – were standing in the long grass of the verge, looking over the thick hawthorn hedge into the field. The children couldn't see any police, but they'd obviously been there, putting out cones to stop people parking both sides. Ben and Midge propped their bikes against the hedge and joined the sightseers.

'I don't see old Dan,' said Ben. 'I thought he'd be on guard with that shotgun of his.'

'No need,' said a man at his side. 'There's a dog.' As he spoke, there was a volley of barking and a border collie came racing along the margin of the field. A man who was leaning on the hedge taking a photograph stepped back hurriedly as the dog thrust its muzzle through a gap, very close to his ankle. Ben laughed. 'Bracken's a sheepdog, not a guard dog. He won't hurt you.'

'Well, I'm not risking it,' said the man who had spoken before. 'And I wouldn't advise anybody else to either. Dogs can be very nasty when they're guarding their territory – even soft dogs. I knew a Pekinese once – a really pampered Pekinese – that put a meter reader in hospital for a month because the fellow stepped inside the house without permission.'

Ben looked at the man. He was a stranger; a tall, thin chap with crinkly hair and a stoop. His story sounded pretty far-fetched – the sort of tale you might tell if you wanted to scare people off. Ben decided to test him. 'Well,' he said. 'I didn't come all this way to stand looking through a hedge. I'm off in.'

'Ben!' Midge made a grab at his arm as he moved forward. She missed, but the stranger didn't. His arm shot out and long, bony fingers closed round Ben's left bicep. 'Steady, lad,' he said, quietly. 'Don't want to be savaged, now do we?'

'Get off me!' Ben, furious, tried to jerk his arm free but the thin man's grip was strong. He bent down and put his lips to Ben's ear. 'Like hospital food, do you?'

'What d'you mean?' Ben's cheeks were scarlet. This bonehead was making him look daft in front of Midge. He twisted and writhed but the man held him easily.

'What do I mean?' he hissed, tightening his grip so that Ben had to grit his teeth to keep from crying out. 'What do I mean? I mean this – that unless you make yourself scarce – unless you skedaddle, right now, taking Olive Oyl here with you – you'll be on hospital food for a long, long time, and for the first few weeks you won't taste it because it'll be going into your arm through a tube. Do you understand what I'm saying?' He squeezed, savagely. 'Do you?'

'Y-yes.'

'All right then.' Some of the sightseers were casting curious glances in their direction. The man let go of Ben's arm. 'Go on,' he murmured. 'Get out of here, and don't ever let me find you near Cansfield land again – either of you.'

'Who the heck was he?' said Midge, as they re-trieved their bikes and turned them towards Little Pitney.

'I don't know,' breathed Ben, glancing back and massaging his bruised arm. 'But I'm going to find out, and when I do I bet he turns out to be a *Daily Telegraph* reader who cooks with tahini.'

It was after ten when the last sightseer returned to his car and drove off, leaving Rex Exley alone on the verge. He gazed balefully after the dwindling vehicle, then walked along to the farm track and turned in, leaving the track at one point to pass the tractor Dan Cansfield had parked across it to discourage visitors. Behind him, the sun was setting in a blaze of glory, and his shadow, enormously long, went before him as he walked. He skirted the house and negotiated a narrow, muddy pathway between outbuildings. Through a doorway he glimpsed Barry, the Cansfields' kid, wielding a shovel. He seemed to be sniffling as he worked, and Exley felt a rare stab of sympathy. He didn't like kids, but had seen enough of Dan Cansfield to feel for any living thing, human or otherwise, that found itself in his power.

When the buildings stopped the path continued, crossing a scrubby bit of pasture where hunks of agricultural machinery lay rusting. Beyond this pasture stood two structures. One was the great, dilapidated barn in which the tank and its ancillary equipment were concealed, and the other was the goose-house, a low stone building in which Wanda Free had her temporary home. Exley stuck his head into the barn to check that the woman wasn't there, then crossed to the goose-house and rapped on its thick, scarred door.

'Yes, who is it?'

There was irritation in Wanda's tone and Exley rolled his eyes heavenward and sighed. 'It's Rex,' he called. 'I'd like a word.'

'All right. Just a minute.'

He waited, watching the rim of the sun go down behind a stand of elms beyond the Warminster Road. A bolt scraped and rattled. The door opened a crack. 'Well?'

Half-blinded from staring into the orange glare, Exley screwed up his eyes. 'I – just to say they've gone, Wanda. The sightseers I mean. I don't think they'll be back. Novelty's worn off, that sort of thing.'

26

The woman nodded. 'No tenacious amateur sleuth, then?'

Exley shrugged. 'There was a kid. Cheeky young beggar of eleven or twelve. Local. Knows the dog. He was all for pushing through the hedge till I grabbed him.' He chuckled. 'Put the fear of God into him, I can tell you. He won't be back.'

'Well, I should hope not, Rex. Anything else?'

'One small point. Is the tank door fastened tonight, Wanda?'

'Now you listen, mister.' The woman's voice was icy. 'I know my job. I don't need you checking up on me because of one itsy-bitsy mistake. You do your job and leave me to do mine.'

'Fine, Wanda. That's fine. I was checking, that's all. We can't be too careful.'

'D'you think I don't know that? A few more days and I'll have the nutrient mix right. Then they won't even want to escape. G'night, Rex.'

The man mumbled goodnight to the closed door, turned, and shuffled through the twilight back towards the house.

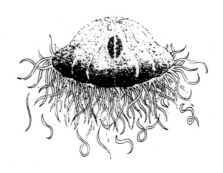

S I X

'Can't you sneak out when your parents are asleep?'
It was lunchtime Wednesday, dry and warm. Barry
Cansfield was still off school. Ben had joined Midge
in her corner of the playground. They were discussing
last night's incident and Ben had just said he'd like
to have a really good snoop round Cansfield Farm.
Midge's suggestion took him by surprise.

'I don't think so, Midge. They'd hear me on the
stairs, or else Dad would be in the kitchen having a
drink when I got back. He gets thirsty in the middle
of the night, my dad.'

'Have you ever tried it – sneaking out, I mean?'

'No.'

'Oh, I have. Lots of times. Everything's different
at night. It's like the whole human race has died out

except you. You sit in the bus shelter and it feels like if you sat there forever there'd be no bus ever again, and nobody'd walk past either. You can think at night, it's so still and quiet.'

Ben giggled. 'You're a nut, Midge. I never knew you did stuff like that. Next time I wake up at night I'll think about you sitting in the bus shelter. What else do you do?'

Midge shrugged her thin shoulders. 'I walk. Sometimes I go in Pitney Wood and look for owls and badgers.'

'Have you ever met anyone while you've been out?'

'No. I've seen PC Aspinall a couple of times but I don't let him see me.'

'And you've never been caught sneaking out?'

'No. Mum and Dad don't close the restaurant till after midnight, and then they've to drive from Warminster, so it's one in the morning by the time they get to bed. They zonk out in seconds, and once they're asleep you could drive a tractor round their room all night and they wouldn't stir.'

'You mean your folks go off to the Forum every night and leave you alone in the house?' Ben was fascinated.

'Oh, yes. Every night except Monday. Monday's their night off. My gran used to come and sit when I was little, but not any more.'

'Wow – you're really lucky, Midge. Wish it was me.'

'Why?'

'Well – all that freedom. I mean, all I get at night is how was school, wash the dishes, be in by nine, tidy your room and no, you can't watch that because your mother and I want to watch so-and-so on Channel Four. It must be absolutely great having the place to yourself.'

Midge smiled. 'They leave me chores to do, Ben, and it's lonely sometimes. When I was little, I'd wake up crying over some dream or something, and they'd be so zonked out they'd never hear. I'd cry for hours sometimes but nobody ever came.'

'Yes, but that was when you were small. It must be great now.'

Instead of replying Midge looked down, rolling a bit of gravel around with the toe of her trainer. 'I'd meet you, come with you if you sneaked out one night.'

Ben was tempted. The thought of leaving the house in the middle of the night was pretty scary, and so was the prospect of creeping around Dan Cansfield's property, but there was a mystery to be solved, and the thought of being out there with Midge gave him a pleasantly queasy feeling which made him gulp. 'OK,' he croaked. 'When?'

Midge smiled again. She looks like that picture when she smiles, thought Ben. The 'Mona Lisa'. 'What's wrong with tonight?'

'Tonight?' Ben couldn't find anything wrong with tonight, except that it was too soon. If they waited a couple of days, something might happen which would explain the strange events at Cansfield Farm, and then they wouldn't need to go at all.

'Yes.' Midge was ruthless. 'Why not tonight? I'll meet you at the bus shelter at half-past one.'

'Half-past one?' He was repeating her words like a parrot but he needed time to think and Midge was giving him none.

'Yes. My folks'll be well away by then.'

'Mine might not be, though. Suppose—'

'Suppose nothing. Half-one. And don't be late – it gets cold in that shelter.'

Ben gazed after Midge as she wandered off. He'd have welcomed some discussion of their plan, but it was too late. She'd forced him into this daunting arrangement and gone off before he could say a word. So. Half-past one it would have to be. He looked at his watch.

Twelve and a half hours from now.

It seemed a long day. Ben couldn't stop thinking about that night. Little videos kept playing themselves inside his head. One was nice. It showed moonlit fields and shadowy woods and two people walking hand in hand. One of them was himself. The other was a fair-haired girl with spindly legs. He sat watching this with glazed eyes and a silly smile while everybody else did maths, but some of the other videos weren't nearly so pleasant.

In one, he was walking stealthily between dark buildings, holding his breath. Suddenly a dog barked, a door flew open and Dan Cansfield was squinting at him along the barrel of a shotgun.

Another was of Midge and himself wading through waist-high wheat. There was no moon and it was very dark. They reached the great circle and stepped on to the mat of flattened stalks. As they did so, a hole appeared at the centre of the circle. The ground on which they were standing tilted towards the hole, which was widening. All around the ground was sinking, so that the circle became a funnel which drew everything in towards the yawning hole, faster and faster. He felt himself sliding in. He grabbed Midge's hand but she was going too, toppling forward—

Walking down the driveway at half-past three, Ben couldn't remember anything they'd done in class that day. Inside his skull the videos rolled on. He couldn't stop them, and though he gave Midge a grin and a conspiratorial wink when they parted in front of Tarkington's Mini-Market, he was more nervous than he had ever been in his life.

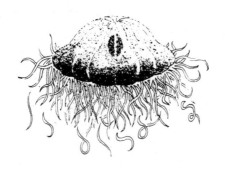

S E V E N

The hard part was staying awake. His bedtime during
the week was nine-thirty, which meant he had to
lie for nearly four hours without nodding off. He
thought of setting his alarm for one-fifteen and getting
some sleep, but it was a fairly loud alarm and it'd
be disastrous if it disturbed his parents. Instead, he
decided to keep his brain active by making a plan
of action for the night, but when he started to think
about this he hit a couple of snags. One, he had
only ever seen Cansfield Farm from a distance, so he
wasn't familiar with the layout of the place. You can't
very well plan your moves if you don't know what
sort of ground you're going to be on or what your
surroundings will be like. And two, he had no clear
idea what he and Midge would be looking for.

Mum's story of the two 'Ts' – *Telegraph* and tahini – suggested there might be a stranger at the farm, and the man who had threatened them last night might be this stranger. But then what? The man had seemed anxious to keep people from getting close to the corn circle. But why? Had he made the circle? Was he perhaps an alien in disguise? And was it likely that he and Midge Fixby would discover anything by prowling about Cansfield Farm in the middle of the night? If the man was staying at the farm he'd be tucked up somewhere fast asleep at two in the morning. They wouldn't see him, and anyway Ben didn't want to. The stranger had hard fingers, and once had been enough. They'd get a close look at the circle, of course, and maybe that would tell them something. If they searched among the buildings they might find – what? An alien craft?

'Oh, I don't know,' sighed Ben. He shook his head to clear it, sat up and peered at the digitalarm on the bedside cabinet. Twenty-three twenty-three. Surely Mum and Dad would be up soon?

They came at twenty to twelve. Ben lay still and closed his eyes in case one of them looked in, but they didn't. After the usual comings and goings between bathroom and bedroom he heard their door close, and within minutes all was silent.

Ben got out of bed and started pulling on his clothes in the green glow from his clock. There was still over an hour to wait but he was horribly tired, and he'd stand more chance of staying awake if he was up.

When he'd finished dressing he sat in the chair by the open window, breathing the cool night air. Wonder what Midge is doing, he mused. Her folks wouldn't even be in yet. Thinking of Midge set the moonlight video playing again and this passed the time, so that when he looked at the clock it was one-fifteen.

He got up, crossed the room on tiptoe, eased open his door and listened. No sound was coming from his parents' room. He slipped out, closed the door carefully and crossed the landing. The stairs creaked a bit and he paused, holding his breath and straining his ears. He was trembling. Hearing nothing he moved on down.

In the hallway he slipped into his jacket and crept through to the kitchen. He daren't leave by the front door. It was under his parents' room and there was a streetlamp near the gate. It'd be just his luck to bump into PC Aspinall. He unlocked the back door and let himself out. This way he'd only to cross a couple of gardens and the pub car park, and the bus shelter would be dead opposite.

'Don't get thirsty, Dad,' he whispered, closing the door. 'And if you do, for goodness sake don't check the back door.'

The night was warm and cloudy. There was no moon. Ben shinned over the fence, crossed next-door's garden and squeezed through the hedge on to the pub car park. There was one car. He watched it for a minute from the shadows. Nobody was in it so he crossed swiftly, dropped to his hands and knees and crawled under the clipped beeches. Once through he rose, turned left and followed the hedge down to the road.

He glanced to his left. High Street stood deserted, bathed in amber light. He looked right, to where the streetlamps stopped and High Street became the Warminster Road. Nothing moved upon it. The only sound was the soft rustle of beech leaves in the breeze.

He looked across, into the black mouth of the shelter. She was there, a pale shape sitting on the bench, watching him with her Mona Lisa eyes. A familiar ache rose in his chest and he swallowed hard as he crossed the road.

'Hi. How long you been here?'

She shrugged. 'Ten, twelve minutes.'

'Am I late, then?' He tried to look at his watch and found it wasn't on his wrist. 'Damn.'

'What?'

'Left my watch.'

'Don't matter. I got mine and you're not late. I was early. C'mon.' Midge got up and peered out. 'OK.' They turned left, hurrying under the last lamp and on into darkness.

No lights burned at Cansfield Farm. From the foot of the track the cluster of buildings was barely visible. Midge said, 'What now?'

Ben pulled a face. 'Have a squint at the circle first, eh?' Now that it was real, he didn't fancy the buildings at all. Getting in among them was going to feel like walking into a trap, but he knew he'd have to do it because Midge was there. If he was by himself he'd chicken out at once, inventing some excuse so he wouldn't feel bad about it. But not in front of Midge. For perhaps the thousandth time he wished that he was brave, but fearlessness wasn't something you got by wishing. So. He'd build up to this thing gradually. The circle first, then the place itself. Obliquely through the wheatfield, not straight up the track. Perhaps he'd have his courage up by then.

They walked back along the hedge and crawled through. It was very dark. Ben peered into the field. 'I'm sure it's just about here.'

'D'you bring a torch?' Midge murmured.

Ben felt a stab of anger and self-contempt. Damn. No watch, no guts and now no torch. What a fantastic impression he must be making on her. He shook his head, dumbly.

' 'S OK – I have.'

Well, you would, wouldn't you? he thought savagely, as Midge rummaged in the big front pocket of her anorak. I bet you've got matches in there too, and a whistle, and emergency rations and a first-aid kit. You came prepared, and I came like somebody going down the corner shop. And I couldn't even get up the nerve to ask to hold your hand coming along.

Midge produced a slim torch. She clicked it on and played its beam back and forth across the rippling wheat. 'I'm not sure that's a good idea, Midge,' whispered Ben. 'What if somebody's looking out, up at the farm?'

Midge snorted. 'It's nearly two in the morning, Ben. Who's going to be looking out?'

Ben shrugged. 'You never know.'

Midge continued to sweep the field with her light, and after a moment she found the edge of the great round depression. 'There it is – look.'

'Yeah.' Ben swallowed. 'OK, let's get a closer look.'

Ben shivered as they stepped into the circle. He remembered a story he'd had read to him in infant school about a kid who stood in a fairy ring and was whisked away to a land inside a hollow hill.

It didn't happen though. The ground didn't tilt and the circle had no hole at its centre. Midge pointed her torch downwards and they saw how the stalks of ripening wheat lay flat against the earth like a dense, neat mat. It was neat because every stalk had fallen the same way and because the circle was perfect, with a sharp clean rim. There were no partly flattened stalks, even near the edge. The mat of horizontal stalks ended abruptly at a wall of vertical ones, and none of the fallen stalks was bruised or broken.

'Wow,' breathed Midge. 'Isn't this weird? Wonder what did it?'

Ben shook his head. 'That's what we're here to find out.' It sounded good, that. It was the sort of thing heroes say on telly, but Ben was wishing he was safe in bed and hoping Midge couldn't read minds.

'OK.' Midge switched off the torch. 'Best get up the farm then, Ben. No answers here.'

'Right,' said Ben, in the flat, clipped tone of the man of action, but his legs shook so badly he nearly fell flat on his face.

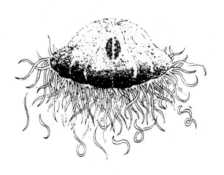

E I G H T

Wanda Free couldn't sleep. She lay on her side in the narrow bed and worried. She worried about the floaters out there in the barn. Their breeding habits. Their longevity. Their diet. Especially their diet. She was sure she had the ingredients right. She ought to have, considering the wealth of data she'd amassed before she walked out on NASA. A series of six probes, the simplest costing a billion dollars and each more sophisticated than the one before, had orbited the giant planet, measuring, analysing, taking pictures. The last two had swooped deep into the atmosphere to capture chemical samples for analysis in on-board autolabs, one of them capturing rather more than its controllers bargained for. Yes, the ingredients were right. Of course they were. Proportions were a bit out of whack, that was all.

All? She groaned, flipped on to her back and stared at the lime-washed ceiling. It's harming them, that imbalance, she thought. Poisoning 'em slowly, and they're the only ones we'll ever see on Earth. The only ones. I can't let them die.

She sat up, peered at the clock on the bedside table. Two-fifteen. Jeez, two-fifteen! She lay down, pulled the duvet up to her chin. Gotta get some sleep. Bet he's sleeping, down there in the house, she thought. She closed her eyes and a picture formed: Rex Exley flat on his back, mouth open, snoring, dead to the world.

What was it he'd said to her, the smug, slimy streak of ooze? Is the tank door fastened tonight, Wanda? As though most nights it wasn't. Well, she'd told him, right? She'd put him firmly in his place before slamming the goose-house door in his simpering mug, thinking, here's one door you can be sure is shut tonight, my friend. Poor old Exley. She smiled briefly in the dark. What he doesn't realize is that I'm in control. Always. There are no screw-ups on my operation. No accidents. Nothing happens without I make it happen, and that goes for doors too. But I wish those nutrients would come right.

She sighed, opened her eyes and threw back the covers. Wanda wasn't fond of burning the midnight oil. She liked her sleep too much. But who was sleeping? Might as well be over there taking another look at the problem. She sat up, snapped on the bedside light and reached for the long white bathrobe she'd draped over the back of the chair.

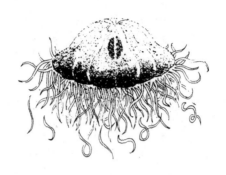

N I N E

They weren't interested in the house. In fact, they'd have preferred to stay well away from it if it had been possible to do so and still get a look at the outbuildings.

It wasn't, and they found themselves creeping along a narrow pathway with the house on their left and a line of ramshackle structures on their right. Some of these buildings had open doors into which Ben and Midge peered as they passed. Others whose doors were fastened had small, dusty windows, but the children dared not risk the torch and saw only blackness through them. The buildings extended well beyond the house, so that by the time they'd investigated the last one, which ponged a bit and proved to house a great, pale bull, it lay some distance behind them.

'Phew!' Ben wiped his brow with his hand and raked his damp hair back. 'That wasn't much fun. I kept expecting Bracken to bark.'

Midge nodded. 'Me too. What now?'

It had been a disappointing reconnaissance. The buildings with open doors contained nothing un-usual, and the others had proved impossible to in-vestigate at all. When he thought about it, Ben saw this as inevitable: if you've got something to hide you don't shove it in an outhouse and leave the door wide open. So. There might be something be-hind one of those locked doors and there might not. Either way, they were none the wiser for their expedition.

'I reckon we've done all we can for tonight.' He managed to inject some disappointment into his voice but his heart soared. All they had to do now was get past the house again and they'd be away. I haven't done too badly after all, he congratulated himself. We came right through the buildings and she's no idea how scared I've been. Maybe she'll let me meet her again some night and we'll do something less dangerous, like sitting in the bus shelter holding hands.

'Hey, just a minute.' Midge was peering along the path, which faded into the dark beyond the bull-pen. 'There's another building over there, Ben. A big one. We might as well take a look.'

Ben's heart sank. 'Right,' he said, briskly. 'This could be what we've been looking for, Midge.' He was about to add 'Follow me,' when Midge set off towards the almost invisible structure with what Ben considered to be unnecessary speed.

It was pitch black on the pathway, and they were halfway there when Ben saw the ghost.

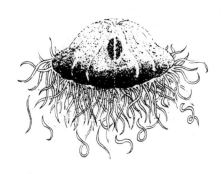

T E N

'Jeez it's cold.' The woman paused in the doorway, clutching the bathrobe tight about her body. 'You don't expect it in July.' She didn't want to leave the goose-house and cross the dewy grass in slippered feet to the barn. She wanted to scuttle right back to her snug bed, but she knew she wouldn't sleep so what was the point?

She'd almost reached the barn when she thought she saw something move between her and it, and it was then she discovered she'd left her torch behind.

E L E V E N

'Midge!' With one eye on the hurrying girl and the other on the apparition gliding in from his left, Ben called out in a harsh, cracked whisper.

'What?' Midge didn't whisper. She didn't stop either.

'Hello?' cried the apparition. 'Who's there?'

Midge turned. 'What's that? Was that you, Ben?'

Ben shook his head, pointing. 'It was that – thing. That ghost.'

Midge saw the white figure, which had stopped and seemed to be watching them. 'Oh, lord!' She ran back, colliding with Ben who stood as though paralysed. 'Run, Ben! Go on, you dummy – get going.'

The apparition was moving fast towards them now. Midge turned Ben and shoved him. Whimpering noises came out of his mouth and he started to run. She aimed her torch at the apparition and switched on. The figure cried out, flung up its arms to shield its eyes.

Midge whirled and ran.

They passed the house, pelted down the track and swung left along the road, not stopping till the lights of Little Pitney came in sight. They stood panting, looking back. 'What the heck was it, Midge?' No use now pretending he hadn't been scared.

Midge shook her head. 'I'm not sure, Ben. A woman I think, in a long white thing.'

'A ghost?'

'Naw. Don't think so. She said, "Hello, who's there?" Ghosts don't say stuff like that, and she looked solid enough when I hit her with the torch.'

Ben gaped. 'You hit her?'

'Not like that, dummy. The beam. I dazzled her with the beam and she sort of yelled out and covered her eyes. A ghost wouldn't do that, would it?'

'Well, who could it have been, then? Not Mrs Cansfield?'

'Doubt it. Not tall enough. Too quick.'

'Who then?'

'I dunno, do I? Another mysterious stranger. The wife of the guy who grabbed you, maybe. Anyway, we'd best get on – it'll be light before long.'

It was true. Already the chimneys of Cansfield Farm were becoming visible, the sky behind them faintly luminous as light from the unrisen sun reflected off the undersides of clouds. A sleepy thrush piped somewhere along the hedge.

'What's the time?'

Midge looked at her watch. 'Twenty-five past two.'

'Crikey! Less than an hour since we started. It seems ages.'

'I told you – everything's different at night.'

They walked on into the comforting luminescence of streetlamps. Now that the danger was past, Ben was beginning to worry about getting back into the house. At least there was no commotion in the High Street, which there surely would have been if his absence had been discovered.

They paused by the bus shelter. Midge gazed along the street looking for PC Aspinall, while Ben gazed wistfully at Midge. Their adventure was almost over and he hadn't even held her hand. He was wondering what she'd do if he reached out and took it now when, suddenly, she turned, kissed him on the cheek and fled, running up Tansy Road while he stood gaping.

There was no further hassle. He took the same route home he'd used on the way out, except that this time he walked on air. The door was as he'd left it and his father hadn't been down. As he slipped between the sheets, his clock read two forty-five.

Ben didn't sleep much, but it wasn't the events at Cansfield Farm he kept replaying in his head. It was that peck on the cheek and the way she'd looked, hurrying away on those thin legs from what she'd done to him.

T W E L V E

'What is it, Wanda?'

It was eight in the morning and Rex Exley had been summoned to the glass and plastic cubicle inside the barn. He didn't like the barn at the best of times and early morning was definitely not the best of times. He hadn't even had breakfast.

'What is it?'

The woman looked tired and sounded irritable. Exley groaned inwardly.

'You might well ask. I was out again last night while you slept.'

'Why? Did the alarm go off?'

'No, the alarm did not go off, but there was some-one prowling around. Two people, I think. They sounded like kids.'

'Kids?' Exley's eyes narrowed. 'A girl and a boy?'

'How would I know, Rex? It was dark. It could've been a girl and a boy, I suppose. Why?'

'That kid. The one I told you about. He'd a girl with him. Thin, anaemic-looking creature with funny eyes. I bet it was them.'

The woman's scarlet mouth warped sarcastically. 'You told me you scared 'em off. Put the fear of God into him, you said.'

'Yes, well—'

'Listen. Somebody's sufficiently interested in what goes on here to come prowling at two in the morning, and that's not good. From now on I want this place guarded, night and day.'

'Guarded? Guarded by whom, Wanda? There's only you and me.'

'There's only you, Rex. I need my rest. Maybe you can fix something with Cansfield and the kid. We're paying them plenty. I don't care how you do it, but I want guards in place from tonight.'

'Tonight? That's a bit—'

'Guards, Rex.' Her voice was icy. 'Armed guards. From tonight. Without fail. That's all.'

Dismissed, he left the barn like a sleepwalker and made his way back to the house where breakfast awaited him. Breakfast was a big meal at Cansfield Farm, but Rex had no appetite now.

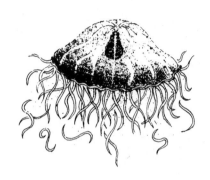

T H I R T E E N

For the third morning in a row there was no churchyard
ambush, but Barry Cansfield answered his name in class
when the teacher called the register. Ms Otterburn
looked up. 'Have you been ill, Barry?'

'Yes, Miss.'

'Better now?'

'Yes, Miss.'

'Have you brought a note from your parents?'

'No, Miss.'

'Why not, Barry?'

'Miss, they never give me one, Miss.'

The teacher sighed. 'I assume your parents do know
the school requires a note to explain absence, Barry?'

'Yes, Miss.'

'Well then, you mention it to them this afternoon

and bring me one tomorrow morning. Will you remember?'

'Yes, Miss.'

He accosted Ben on the field at break, when Ben was looking for Midge.

'You were laughing, Locky.'

'When?'

'When Rotterburn was on about a note. I saw you.'

'I wasn't Barry, honest. What's been wrong with you anyhow?'

'None of your business. Why'd you laugh?'

'I told you – I didn't. I was thinking about something else.'

'Oh – what?'

'Corn circles.'

Something flickered briefly in Barry's eyes and Ben spotted it. It looked almost like fear.

'Load of rubbish, that.'

Barry was uncomfortable though. Ben decided to push his luck.

'There's one at your place though.'

'Hooligans playing silly boggers.'

'Aliens, Wayne Daykin reckons.'

'Wayne Daykin's a creepazoid.'

'Yes, but they are funny, aren't they? Mysterious.'

'No, they're not.'

'I think so.' Ben was feeling braver all the time. 'In fact, I'm really interested. Would you let me come up your place so I can look at the one in your field?'

'No way. And don't you go telling nobody I've been talking about circles 'cause I haven't. I don't believe in 'em.'

Ben was exultant. The bully didn't seem half so keen to pick a fight now. He decided to push it a bit harder. 'Who you got staying up home, Barry?'

'What d'you mean?'

'Who's staying with you? I know there's somebody 'cause I know someone who's seen 'em.'

'No, you don't. There's nobody 'cept me and my folks.'

'Tall, thin guy. Talks posh. Walks bent over like this.'

'No.'

'Shortish woman. Younger'n your mum. Not from these parts.'

Barry gazed at Ben, and there was no doubt now about the fear.

'There's nobody, right? I never said there was and I never said nowt about circles neither. I've kept my mouth shut. I have.' He spun on his heel and hurried off, and before Ben could resume his search for Midge, the bell rang.

F O U R T E E N

'I need a note, Mum. For school.'

'Better ask your dad, son.'

'Dad. Teacher wants a note.'

'What? Whinin' again, boy? What's it this time?'

'A note, Dad. 'Cause I been off.'

'Buckle-end, eh? That what you want – buckle-end o' my belt?'

'No, Dad. Just a note, for school.'

'Buckle-end, that's what you're asking for, isn't it?'

'No, Dad, I've got to take—'

'What? What you got to take – your trousers down? Is that it?'

'No, Dad, please.'

'What, then?'

'Nothing, Dad.'

'Mum?'
'What is it, Midge?'
'There's this boy at school. Ben Lockwood. I—'
'Not now, Midge, please. Daddy and I are very late as it is. Did anybody phone last night?'
'No, Mum. I just wanted—'
'To talk. I know, Midge. It seems that whenever we're running late, you want to talk. Now don't forget to do the dishes and feed Buster. There's fish for him in the fridge and pizza for your supper. If Gran rings, tell her I'll try to call round Saturday, and I've left a cheque under the clock in case the insurance man comes. If you go out, be sure and be in by nine, and don't stay up too late. 'Bye darling.'
' 'Bye, Mum.'

'How was school today, Ben?'
'OK, Dad.'
'No worries – nothing bothering you?'
'No.'
'It's just that – well, your mother says you've seemed preoccupied lately. A bit quiet. We wondered whether there was something you'd like to talk about.'
It was Thursday, and Ben's mother had left for the library.
'Nothing, Dad. Everything's fine, honestly.' It was, too. His mention of corn circles had subdued Barry

Cansfield in a way which seemed miraculous, and if that continued to work nothing else mattered. There was the mystery, of course, which he intended to pursue in spite of the tall stranger's warning, but he needn't involve his parents in that. As long as Midge was with him, he needed nobody else. And that was another good thing. Midge. Tonight. So yes, everything was fine.

'I'm glad about that, Ben. You do know you can talk to us at any time, don't you? About anything?'

'Yes, Dad.'

What you nattering on about, Dad?

F I F T E E N

It was easier the second time. For one thing, they weren't going up Cansfield. They were meeting because they liked each other's company. Because they wanted to be alone together and night was the best time for that. They'd meet at the bus shelter and stay there unless they decided to go for a walk, so there was no danger. No real danger, anyway. He'd get done, of course, if his parents caught him, but that was nothing compared to the white ghost. The tall stranger. Hospital food.

His parents tended to go to bed earlier, too, on Thursdays. Ben supposed his mother was tired from her evening at the library. Anyway, it meant they'd be that much sounder asleep when it was time for him to move.

It went without a hitch. There were no cars in the pub car park and no sign of PC Aspinall. Midge wasn't in the shelter when he got there but she arrived two minutes later. He knew it was two minutes because this time he'd remembered his watch.

'Hi.'

'Hi, Midge. Glad you could make it.'

'I can always make it. Any hassle your end?'

'Naw.'

They sat on the bench. Midge was swinging her legs. It was dark in the shelter and her white socks seemed to flash each time her feet swung out. Ben watched them. 'What if Aspinall looks in?'

Midge smiled. 'He's got steel tips on his heels. You hear him a mile off. I usually go behind the bushes till he passes.' She giggled.

'Once, he came in the bushes too, for a pee. I bet he'd have died if he'd known I was there.'

Ben laughed. 'I bet he would.'

He didn't know what to say after that, so they sat in silence for a while. A car whizzed by heading for Warminster, and Ben thought how the driver would never know he'd passed within three metres of two kids sitting in a bus shelter at two in the morning. It was a terrific feeling: like being invisible. He looked at Midge.

'You're right, Midge. Everything is different at night.'

She nodded. 'Good, isn't it?'

They fell silent again. Ben listened for steel tips and

heard nothing. The silence almost seemed to hum, like a faraway motor. After a minute he said, 'What d'you think's making them circles, Midge?'

She shook her head. 'Dunno. Something they're doing up Cansfield, I expect. Secret weapon, maybe.'

'D'you think they're Army, then?'

'Could be – undercover like.'

'Why Cansfield though? Army got their own places.'

'Well, I dunno, do I? Spies then, in the pay of a foreign power.'

'Why would spies make circles in the corn?'

'Don't ask me. P'raps its aliens, like Wayne Daykin says.'

'I tried getting Barry on about it but he wouldn't. I think he's scared.'

'Scared? Barry? Nothing scares him, not even teachers.'

'Well, he seemed nervous, y'know, like he'd been told not to say anything.'

'Hmm.' Midge looked thoughtful. 'I wonder if that's why he's been off school?'

'Could be, couldn't it? Something happens up there they don't want talked about so they keep him home. And warn him not to talk. It's got to be something pretty big, Midge, don't you think?'

'Seems like it, yes.'

'D'you think we should tell someone?'

'Like who?'

Ben shrugged. 'Our folks. The police.'

'What would we tell 'em? That some guy warned us

off? That we saw a ghost? That Barry Cansfield seems nervous? The place is thick with nutcases raving about corn circles, Ben. We'd just get laughed at.'

'So, what do we do?'

Midge stopped swinging her legs and looked sideways at him. 'Well, we've got a choice, haven't we? We can do some more investigating, or we can drop it. It's nothing to do with us, after all. You had enough?'

Ben shook his head. 'I want to carry on if you'll help me, only I'm not sure what our next move should be.'

'Aren't you?' Midge grinned. 'Well, I am. It's the people, Ben. We leave the circles for now and investigate the people. The strangers. Listen.'

They sat for another ten minutes while Midge explained her plan. No more vehicles went by and PC Aspinall must have been busy elsewhere. It was twenty past two when they said goodnight, and half-past when Ben got into bed. He slept at once, unaware that less than a mile away a man was sitting with a loaded shotgun across his knees, thinking about him.

S I X T E E N

'Guardin'? There wasn't nothing about guardin' in our agreement, Mr Exley.'

'No, I realize that, Mr Cansfield, but you see the situation's changed. Somebody's snooping around and Ms Free insists that the place be guarded. I did it myself last night, but obviously I can't do it every night or I'll die from exhaustion. What I'm suggesting is a three-way roster – me one night, you the next, then your lad here, then me again. Two nights' sleep in three. What d'you say?'

'Well, I dunno, Mr Exley. There'd have to be something in it for me. Nobody works for nothin', do they, and we're talking about night work. Double time and all that. D'you want more coffee?'

'Ah – yes, that'd be very nice. Thank you.'

'Frieda – more coffee for Mr Exley, and I'll have a warm-up myself. Jump to it now. And you, boy – what you sittin' there for? Time you was off to school, I reckon.'

'Yes, Dad. I was just off.'

'In the cup, woman, not the dad-blasted saucer. I dunno – can't get nothin' done right round here 'less I does it my damn self. Now, what were we saying, Mr Exley?'

'Guarding, Mr Cansfield, and money. I was talking about guarding and you were talking about money, but you know, we're paying you quite handsomely as it is. Enough to include one night in three on guard, I'd say.'

'Two, Mr Exley. Two nights in three. You're forgetting the boy.'

'Two in three then. Even so, I think—'

'And another thing, Mr Exley. There's something as bothers me about all this.'

'Oh? And what might that be, Mr Cansfield?'

'Well, giving you and the young woman a quiet spot to work in's one thing. Having folks snooping round the property in the middle of the night's another. How do I know it ain't police? Secret Service? I can't afford to get tangled up with fellers of that sort, y'know.'

'I can assure you, Mr Cansfield, that neither the police nor the Secret Service is involved here. The work Ms Free and I are doing is secret, but it is not unlawful, neither does it threaten national security. These intruders are merely local busybodies who've been attracted by the so-called corn circles. As soon as they know we're armed and watching, you won't see them for dust.'

'Aah, well. I dunno. I'm startin' to wonder exactly what it is you're doing in my barn, Mr Exley. All that paraphernalia. Alarms in the night, and now snoopers. What you two got in there, eh?'

'I can't tell you, Mr Cansfield, not exactly, because I don't really know myself. Ms Free is the scientist in this partnership. I just provide the cash and look after the ordinary, everyday side of things. And anyway, under the terms of our agreement, what happens in that barn is none of your concern.'

'Ah, but 'tis you that's wantin' to break the terms of our agreement, Mr Exley, with your guardin' and that. And anyway, any livestock on my farm's my business, I'd say.'

'Livestock, Mr Cansfield? Have I said anything about livestock?'

'Don't have to, Mr Exley. I might be just an old farmer but I ain't daft. You got livestock in my barn all right. I seen it one night when I couldn't sleep, see? And we're not talkin' cows nor pigs nor sheep neither. We're talkin' special stock. Imported, you might say, from a long ways off. Now I know a man who'd be very interested in stock like that. Big money, he'd pay, if I was to tell 'im all about it. Bigger than you're paying, and he wouldn't want me standin' guard two nights in three neither, losin' my sleep. So I think you and me better renegotiate, Mr Exley, if it's all the same to you.'

S E V E N T E E N

'Hello? Is this Cansfield Farm, Little Pitney?'

'Yes. Frieda Cansfield speaking. Who am I speaking to?'

'It's Julian. May I speak to my father, please? It's urgent.'

'Are you sure you have the right number, dear – I don't think I know you.'

'This is Cansfield Farm, isn't it? My father's supposed to be staying there.'

'Ah – your father's Rex Exley, is that right?'

'Yes, that's right, Mrs Cansfield. Is he there? I'm on a payphone and I've no more twenties.'

'He's somewhere outside, dear – hang on and I'll fetch him.'

Ben heard a hollow thud as Frieda Cansfield dropped

the receiver. He hung up, scribbled Rex Exley in his jotter and left the phone booth, smiling.

E I G H T E E N

If you were a kid in Little Pitney, the Village Hall was the place to be Saturday mornings. Kids' Koffee Korner, ten till twelve. Coffee, Coke and all the latest sounds. Midge knew there was a good chance Barry would be there and he was, lounging with his cronies at a corner table.

'Hi, Barry.'

' 'Lo, Midge. Where's Locky the wimp then?'

'How should I know? I'm not his mummy.'

The boys laughed, as she'd known they would. Barry gave Ginger Deeping a shove which sent him sprawling on the floor and offered his chair to Midge. 'Siddown. Have a Coke. My treat.' He looked at Wayne Daykin. 'Get her a Coke.'

'Hey!' Midge giggled. 'I thought it was your treat?'

'It is. I'm treating you to a Coke on Daykin's dosh.'

'Gee, thanks a lot, Barry.' She sat down. 'Listen. Something really weird happened to me just now, biking past your place.'

'I know.' Ginger Deeping, cross-legged on the floor, grinned up at her. 'You saw these little green men in the cornfield, right?'

'Shut it, Ginger, OK?'

'Sure, Barry. I was joking, that's all.'

Barry looked at Midge. 'What was it?'

Midge pulled a face. 'You'll think I'm barmy.'

'Try me.'

'Well, I've got this auntie, right? My mum's sister. I've only seen her about four times in my life because she has this very secret job and she's away all the time. Anyway, I'm biking past your place and I see her turning up your track. I'm going pretty fast mind, and anyway it can't be her, but it looks exactly like her and it gives me this really weird feeling, y'know?'

Barry nodded, leaned towards her. 'This auntie – her name Wanda, by any chance?'

'Yes, that's right. Auntie Wanda. How'd you know that, Barry?'

'And her second name's Free, am I right?'

'That's amazing, Barry! You mean you actually know my Auntie Wanda? She visits your place?'

Barry's smile was smug. 'She's staying. Been there weeks. Wouldn't have got the name right else, would I?' He frowned. 'She never mentioned you though, nor your mum.'

'Well, she wouldn't, would she? Secret work, see.
We're not supposed to know where she is. Hey?'

'What?'

'You won't – tell her, will you? That I saw her:
told you all about her job and that. I'd get in awful
trouble if you did.'

'You can trust me, Midge.' He winked. 'Old Barry
knows when to keep his trap shut, eh?'

Midge, head bowed over her Coke can, looked at
him through fair lashes and spoke round a pink and
white straw. 'I know that, Barry,' she said.

NINETEEN

'So he wants more money, is that it?'

Exley nodded. 'That's what it amounts to, yes. He's using the guard duty thing as an excuse, but I think he was getting ready to put the squeeze on us anyway. He knows we've got something alive in that tank and that it's a very hot property. People are getting curious, the pressure's on and he reckons we'll cough up to keep him quiet.'

'And will we?'

Exley shrugged. 'I don't see we've much option, Wanda. He's quite prepared to blow this thing wide open if we turn him down.'

'And next time?'

'What d'you mean, next time?'

'Well, if we give him what he's asking for, what's

to stop him demanding more next week and the week after and so on?'

'Yes, I see what you mean.' He looked at her. 'So what do you suggest?'

The woman didn't answer straight away. She sat with her hands clasped on the desktop, gazing at the tank through the cubicle's tinted window. Her mouth was a thin line and her eyes were hard. After a minute she said, 'Pay him, but throw a scare into him as well. Tell him—' She sat back, moved her hands into her lap and smiled. 'Tell him accidents can happen in our sort of work. Nasty ones. I think he'll understand.'

T W E N T Y

The bus squealed to a juddering stop by the shelter.
Four people got on, leaving Ben and Midge in pos-
session of the bench. As the vehicle drew away, Ben
grinned triumphantly and pulled the jotter from his
pocket. 'It worked, Midge, just like you said. His
name's Rex Exley and he is staying at Cansfield.'

'Well, there you are then.' Midge smiled. 'And I
found out about our ghost. She's called Wanda Free
and she's staying too. All we've got to do now is
find out where they're from and what they're doing
in Little Pitney.'

'D'you think that'll be easy, Midge?'

She shrugged. 'I dunno. Depends how well known
they are. What we'll do is, we'll take the next bus into
Warminster and visit the *Journal*.'

Ben looked at her. 'The *Journal*? Why?' The *Journal* was the town's daily paper.

'Newspapers have libraries, Ben. They keep all the back numbers there, and thousands of clippings neatly filed away. The librarian at the *Journal* is Mrs Tattersall and she knows me, because she and her husband eat at the Forum a lot. I'll give her the names and ask if she's got anything about them. It's worth a try.'

'What if she asks why you want to know?'

'School project. Anyway, she probably won't ask.'

There wouldn't be another bus for twenty-five minutes, so the pair decided to set off and walk two or three stops. Their walk took them past Cansfield Farm, but no vehicles were parked at the roadside and there were no sightseers. The circle was still there, but weeds had begun to grow through the flattened stems, blurring its outline. There were no Cansfields around, and no mystery guests. They were between stops when they heard the bus but they ran, and Ben stuck his hand out just in time.

Mrs Tattersall was incurious and helpful. 'Rex Exley?' she exclaimed, the moment Midge mentioned the name. 'I don't need to look him up, my dear – not if it's the same Rex Exley. He's a big newspaper man, or he was. Owned the Northminster Press Group. Twenty, thirty papers, all over the country. The *Journal*'s one of them.'

'But he doesn't own them now?'

'No. Sold up three, four years ago for umpteen

million pounds. Life of ease now, I expect. Bahamas. South of France '

'And Wanda Free?'

The woman looked dubious. 'Wanda Free? You sure someone's not having you on, dear? It's a funny name if it's genuine.'

'Oh, it's quite genuine, Mrs Tattersall.'

'Well, all I can say is the poor girl's parents had a wicked sense of humour. Wait here and I'll have a look.'

The woman disappeared beyond some iron fixtures stacked with bound back numbers. Ben and Midge waited, whispering, elbows propped on the little counter.

'What's a millionaire ex-newspaperman doing at Cansfield Farm?'

Midge pulled a face. 'Dunno. Maybe it's not the same guy.'

' 'Course it is. How many Rex Exleys can there be? Rex. It's a dog's name.'

'And Ben's a hamster's.'

'Well, Midge is a little fly, so there.'

'Grow up, Ben.'

'Belt up, Midge.'

'Nothing, my dears. Not a sausage. As far as the Warminster *Journal* is concerned, Wanda Free does not exist. She's a figment. A chimera. An unperson.'

'Oh.' Midge looked crestfallen and Mrs Tattersall was quick to console.

'One of the big papers might have something on

her, Midge. The nationals. I could ring a friend of mine on the *Guardian* if you like.'

'Oh, would you, Mrs Tattersall? Please?'

The woman smiled. 'Of course I will, my dear. Not today though. He doesn't work Saturdays. I'll make a note for myself and call him Monday. All right?'

'Yes, thank you, Mrs Tattersall. Shall we come after school Monday, then?'

'Oh, I shouldn't come all this way, dear. There might not be anything, you see. Give me a ring about half-past four. Number's on this card.'

Outside, Midge smiled. 'Not a bad start, eh, Ben? Two days, we've cracked one mysterious stranger and we're after the other.'

'It's you, Midge,' murmured Ben. 'You're a genius.'

Midge grinned. 'I'm not bad, am I? For a little fly, I mean.'

T W E N T Y - O N E

'Oh, Mr Exley.' Frieda Cansfield, aproned and clutching a yellow duster, caught him as he left the barn. His
mind was on the scare he meant to give her husband
along with the money and her voice startled him. 'Mrs
Cansfield. Is something the matter?'

'I'm terribly sorry, Mr Exley, but you see I couldn't
find you and when I went to tell him, he'd rung off,
and then what with one thing and another it went clear
out of my mind.'

'What did, Mrs Cansfield? What're you talking
about?'

'Your son, Mr Exley. Julian. He phoned this morning from a callbox. He said it was urgent but I couldn't
find you and he had no more twenties and when I went
back he'd gone.'

'Son, Mrs Cansfield? I have no son.'

'Oh, but he said— It was a young lad and he said he was your son. He wanted to speak to you urgently. I went to get you and while I was gone—'

'Yes, yes I know, Mrs Cansfield. You've told me all that, but I'm trying to tell you that I have no son, so obviously this chappie was some sort of imposter. What exactly did he say?'

'Well, I don't rightly remember, sir. Not word for word.'

'Did he ask for me by name?'

'Well, no. He asked to speak to his father, and I'd not heard you mention a son so I asked him if his father was Mr Exley and he said yes.'

'Oh, lord. So you gave him my name. What else did you tell him?'

'Nothing, Mr Exley. He didn't ask me anything else. I'm really sorry, sir, but how was I to know he wasn't who he said he was?'

The man shook his head. 'You weren't, Mrs Cansfield. Nobody's blaming you. Excuse me.'

She gazed after him with troubled eyes as he hurried back to the barn.

'Barry. Can I have a word?'

'Yes, Mr Exley.' The boy set down the pail he was carrying and approached, a scrubbing brush in his left hand.

'I understand you're our sentry for tonight, Barry.'

'Oh, yes, sir.'

77

'D'you mind?'

'Pardon?'

'D'you mind being up all night? Staying awake?'

'No, sir.'

'Good lad. You know somebody's been prowling around at night, don't you?'

'Yes, sir. My dad said.'

'And somebody phoned your mother today, pretending to be my son?'

'Yes, sir. Dad give my mum seven kinds of 'ell over that, sir.'

'Did he now? Well, it wasn't really your mother's fault, lad. Anyway, what I'm saying is we're being probed, Barry. Spied upon. Ms Free is quite concerned. She thinks our enemies are closing in, and she wants you to keep an especially sharp lookout tonight. Will you do that?'

'Yes, sir.'

'Good man!' He reached out awkwardly and ruffled the boy's coarse hair. 'I knew we could count on you, Barry.'

Barry smirked. 'So it's secret work, eh, sir? Even 'er own sister don't know she's here.'

'Sister? Whose sister?' Again the journalist reached out, this time grabbing Barry by the shoulders. 'What are you talking about, laddy?'

'Nothing.' Barry writhed under the man's bony grip while his eyes grew wide with fear. He'd gone too far and he knew it. 'I didn't mean nothing Mr Exley, honest. Let me go, you're hurting.'

Exley's grip tightened. 'What's this about a sister? Whose sister? Ms Free's?'

'Yes, sir. I mean no. I was just kidding, Mr Exley. I don't know nothing about a sister, honest.' Barry began to sob and Exley shook him.

'Listen, lad. Either you give me straight answers to my questions, or I get your father to ask them. Would you prefer that?'

'No!'

'Then talk.'

Barry talked. As Exley listened, his lips became compressed to thin, bloodless strips, his cheeks grew pale and his eyes glinted narrowly like slivers of ice. 'Midge Fixby, you say?'

'Yessir. Don't tell my dad, sir. He'll kill me.'

Exley ignored the plea. 'This girl claimed she saw her aunt in the driveway and you mentioned Ms Free's name. Is that it?'

'Yessir. I didn't know, did I? She tricked me.'

'What else did you tell her?'

'Nothing else, sir.'

'Oh, God!' He shoved the weeping boy away from him. 'Go on. Stop blubbing and get about your business. And stay awake tonight or your father will hear of this.'

Barry retrieved his pail and shuffled, shoulders heaving, into an outbuilding. Exley turned and, with a heavy sigh, trudged once more towards the barn.

T W E N T Y - T W O

Barry walked slowly down the rutted driveway. It was a warm, moonlit night, but the shotgun was heavier than it looked. It was making his arm ache. He reached the gateway, propped the weapon against a post and looked at his watch. 00.49. Why does time drag when you want it to pass? he wondered. He stifled a yawn and looked back at the house, which was in darkness. Everybody was asleep. The security of Cansfield Farm was in his hands.

A vehicle was approaching. He heard its motor and stood by the gatepost, very still. It wouldn't be snoopers, of course. They would come more stealthily, but whoever it was it was better they shouldn't see him. It might be a police car.

Headlamps swept the hedge like a searchlight in

a prisoner-of-war movie and the car flashed by on hissing tyres. Barry recognized it and flung a string of insults at its dwindling lights. It was a Saab, the only one in Little Pitney, and it belonged to Karen and Richard Fixby whose only child was Midge.

Midge Fixby. He tucked the gun under his arm and started back up the track. Too clever for her own good, that one. She'd made a monkey out of him, but he'd got her back all right. That prat Exley knew she was a snooper now, so she'd better watch out. He was posh, that Exley, with a quiet way of talking, but behind it all was a cold, hard man you wouldn't want for an enemy.

When Exley and the woman had first arrived at Cansfield, Barry had been glad of their presence. It had modified his father's behaviour, so that for a time he'd shouted less at his wife and there'd been fewer beatings for Barry. Neither of them knew why the two strangers had come, but it was obvious Dan Cansfield was being paid handsomely for playing host, because the farmer had been in jovial mood. Barry had never seen this side of his father before. He'd often wondered how his mother had come to marry such a surly, brutal creature and, for a short time that spring, he fancied he glimpsed the man she'd once loved.

It hadn't lasted, this change for the better. It had soon become obvious that, though they were living cheek by jowl with the family, neither Exley nor Free was the slightest bit concerned about anything that went on in the Cansfield household. Dan Cansfield could have lured passers-by up to the house, cut their throats and buried them under the kitchen floor and the guests wouldn't have turned a hair. So, gradually, things had returned to normal till Dan was bawling out his cringing wife and smacking his son round the head while the strangers looked on.

'I hate 'em,' growled Barry, as he trudged up the side of the house. 'All of 'em, with their money and their rotten little secret. None of 'em give a damn . about me except Mum, and she can't do nothing. They're all fast asleep in there, dreaming of fame and fortune, and here's me trailing about in the middle of the night guarding it for 'em. And what do I get out of it? The buckle-end of Dad's belt, that's what. Well, I'll show 'em. One of these days I'll find a way of getting 'em back.'

TWENTY-THREE

On the bus back from Warminster, Ben tried to fix a meeting with Midge for the following day. He said they could discuss events so far and make plans for the next phase of the investigation, though really he just wanted to see her. He was doomed to disappointment though, because Midge told him her parents were taking her to Longleat for the day.

'Longleat?' cried Ben. 'Have you never been there?'

'Oh, yeah,' said Midge. 'Several times.'

'But you're crazy about lions, right?'

Midge smiled. 'Dad is. It's him wants to go really but he needs me as an excuse. You know – like those adults who love jelly babies but pretend they're buying them for a kid.'

'Ah, right. Still, it's the last week of school. Plenty of time in the holidays, eh?'

Midge nodded. 'Six weeks. We'll crack this mystery wide open in that time, Ben.'

So Ben spent Sunday by himself. He gave Michaelangelo's tank a thorough clean, went to church with his mother, oiled and polished his bike and took a long, slow walk through Pitney Wood to think. He thought about Midge, of course, and hoped she was having a good time at Longleat. He thought about Rex Exley, but mostly he thought about Wanda Free. Who was she? What was she? What would Mrs Tattersall find out? Roll on tomorrow, he whispered, which wasn't like Ben at all.

' 'Bye, Mum.' Leaving for school that Monday morning, Ben felt vaguely apprehensive. Things've been going too well, he told himself. Midge. The investigation. Hols coming up. Something's bound to go wrong and I bet I know what it'll be. It'll be Barry. He'll be lurking in the churchyard right now, back to his old tricks. He'll grab me and give me a king-size duffing-up to make up for the ones I've missed.

He was wrong. Nobody was in the churchyard. The morning sun warmed the mossy stones, the yews were alive with birds, and there seemed to be flowers everywhere.

School dragged like he knew it would, but that was all. Barry wasn't even there. He didn't see Midge at break, but she was waiting for him on the drive at half-past three.

'Hi, Midge. How were the lions?'

Midge shrugged. 'Lion around as usual.'

Ben groaned at the feeble joke and Midge grinned. 'We only caught a glimpse of them in the distance, Ben. It was a baboon day mostly.'

'How d'you mean?'

Midge pulled a face. 'They came swarming all over the car, and one actually stuck its bum up against the windscreen and kept it there for ages. I thought I'd die.' She giggled. 'It was like you looking in, Ben.'

'Thanks a lot. Where are we making this phone call from – your place?'

She shook her head. 'Mum'll be there. I thought we'd use the box outside Tarkington's. Got any coins?'

Ben searched his pockets. 'A fifty, a twenty and two tens.'

Midge nodded. 'And I've got two twenties, so we're laughing. It's a bit early, mind. She did say half-past four.'

'I know, but she'll have done it by now, and if she hasn't we can ring again.'

'OK, we'll give it a go.'

There was a man in the phone-box. It was ten to four when he came out. He was a stranger, and Ben gave him a malevolent glare all the way to his car before joining Midge.

'Hello? Is that Mrs Tattersall? Oh, it's Midge, Mrs Tattersall. I'm sorry I'm a bit early but – right. Oh, great! Just a minute – I'd better get something to write on.'

Ben had been waiting for this. Hoping for it. He pulled jotter and pencil from his pocket and slid them under Midge's hand, feeling he was making up for his unpreparedness of the other night. Midge flashed him a quick smile and said, 'Right, I'm ready. She's what? How d'you spell it? E–X–A, and then biologist? Right. Ah-ha. Ah-ha. Right.' The pencil jiggled slant-wise across the jotter. Ben craned over the girl's thin shoulder, trying to read the information as it appeared, but the handwriting was awful.

'Ah-ha. Did he? What sort of mystery? Ah. No. No, we're doing this scientific investigation and we came across her name, that's all. No, no trouble, Mrs Tattersall, really. If it was anything like that we'd – yes, straightaway.' Midge laughed and wrinkled up her nose at Ben. 'We're no heroes, Mrs Tattersall. We'd run a mile if— No. Yes. Well, thanks a lot, Mrs Tattersall, that's terrific. And thank your friend for us too. Yes, I will. Thanks. 'Bye.'

'What'd she say?'

'Hang on, Ben. I want to write this down before I forget.' Midge scribbled for a while then paused, chewing the end of the pencil then scribbling some more. 'Right. I think that's all. Come on.'

They left the box and walked on, past Ben's house and the end of Tansy Road to the bus shelter, which was unoccupied. They sat down.

'What'd she say, Midge?'

Midge smiled. 'Wanda Free's a scientist, Ben. An exabiologist, whatever that means. She's British, but she's been in America for years and years, working on the space programme. She was employed by NASA, and worked at something called the Jet Propulsion Laboratory, but Mrs Tattersall's friend says she had some sort of bust-up with NASA about a year ago and vanished. It was all hushed up, but he reckons NASA would give a lot to know where she is right now, and what she's doing.'

'Wow! And we know, Midge. You and me. Where she is, anyway.'

Midge nodded. 'This guy told Mrs Tattersall to warn whoever was asking that they might be getting into something dangerous. She asked me what we were doing and were we in trouble of any kind. I said we were doing scientific investigation, like it was part of our schoolwork. I said we weren't heroes and if we hit anything dodgy we'd go to an adult with it. She made me promise, Ben.'

'And do you think we've hit something dodgy, Midge?'

Midge smiled, her Mona Lisa smile.

'Not that dodgy,' she said. 'Not yet.'

T W E N T Y - F O U R

'Mum?'

'What?' His mother was chopping lettuce.

'What's an exabiologist?'

'An exabiologist? I don't know, dear. I know what a biologist is, but I don't know about the "exa" bit. Where've you come across that?'

'School.'

'And doesn't your teacher know?'

'Didn't ask.'

'You could try the dictionary.'

'I have. It's not in. D'you think Dad might know?'

'Possibly. You can ask him when he gets in. D'you want a bit of this for Michaelangelo?'

Ben took a handful of chopped lettuce and went out to the shed. He dropped the lettuce into the tank then bent his knees to watch the little creature through the glass. Michaelangelo stood on his hind legs with a bit of the greenery clasped in his forepaws and munched busily. 'Hey, Mick,' said Ben. 'Do you know what an exabiologist is?'

When he heard the car, Ben put the cover on the tank and returned to the house.

'Hi, Dad.'

'Hello, Ben. How was school?'

'Useless.'

'What d'you mean, useless?'

'Well, nobody could tell me what "exabiologist" means.'

'You said you didn't ask,' protested his mother.

'I asked you though, and the dictionary, and Michael-angelo. Nobody knows. You're my last hope, Dad.'

'An exabiologist,' said his father smugly, 'is one who studies alien life-forms – creatures which do not originate on Earth. In other words, little green men.'

Ben stared at him. 'Are you kidding, Dad?'

'Certainly not, Ben. You asked me a serious question and I've answered it, seriously. That's what an exabiologist is.'

'But there are no alien life-forms, Dad. Not that we know of.'

'That's true, Ben.'

'So what do they study for Pete's sake – nothing?'

'Now that I can't tell you, son, but I imagine they look at conditions on other planets – temperatures, composition of atmosphere if any, gravity and so forth, and try to decide whether life could exist there, and if so what sort of life.'

'I sometimes wonder that about Little Pitney,' said Ben's mother, and both his parents started laughing.

Ben didn't feel like laughing. What if he told them there was an exabiologist at Cansfield Farm? That'd stop 'em laughing, wouldn't it? No it wouldn't, he told himself. They'd probably start on about flying pigs or purple sheep or five-legged cows or something. You might as well not tell adults anything. If you do, they always end up laughing.

'Dad?'

'Yes, Midge?'

'What's an exabiologist?'

'I haven't the foggiest idea, love. Ask your mother.'

'I did. She said to ask you.'

'Pass me that disk, will you, love? Ta. Have you looked it up?'

'Yes. It's not in.'

'Oh.'

'So how do I find out, Dad?'

'Ask your teacher.'

'But that's tomorrow. I want to know now.'

'Look, Midge. We can't always do just what we want to do, just when we feel like doing it. Now run along, because I want to finish updating this stocklist before your mum and I go out.'

'Yes, Dad. Thanks.'

T W E N T Y - F I V E

'Midge. I've been looking all over for you. Listen. D'you know what an exabiologist is?'

'Sssh!' Midge looked about her. 'Keep your voice down, Ben, for goodness sake. Somebody might hear.'

It was breaktime Tuesday. He'd found her, alone as usual, behind the bike sheds. He grinned. 'Nobody comes round here, Midge. That's why you're here. Do you know what an exabiologist is?'

'No. I tried the dictionary but it wasn't in.'

'Your mum and dad?'

'They weren't in either. If you know, why don't you just tell me?'

He told her.

'So.' She looked down, drawing invisible patterns

91

on the tarmac with the toe of her trainer. 'What do we know?'

'Huh?'

'What do we know, Ben?' She spread her left hand and counted off points on her fingers. 'One. Two strangers are staying at Cansfield Farm. Two. One's a rich ex-newspaper man and the other's an exabiologist. Three. An exabiologist studies alien life-forms. Four. Corn circles have appeared lately on Cansfield land and our mysterious strangers seem nervous about them. Five—' She paused, frowning. 'Well, this isn't something we know exactly, but it makes sense. Five. The corn circles have something to do with alien life-forms.'

Ben ran his tongue across his lower lip. 'You mean – you're saying Wayne Daykin's right, Midge? The circles are made by aliens?'

The girl nodded. 'Looks like it, doesn't it?'

'You think alien craft have landed?' His voice was croaky. 'You reckon they're going to invade, Midge?'

Midge shook her head. 'Not necessarily. It needn't be craft, even.'

'How d'you mean?'

'Well – the circles could be made by the aliens themselves, couldn't they? With feet, I mean. Or bodies. Those two might have some aliens hidden on the farm.'

'But even so, they'd have to arrive in a craft of some sort, wouldn't they?'

Midge looked at him. 'Probably, yes. But it might have been one of ours, Ben.'

'Ours? But we don't have—'

' 'Course we do.'

'Well, yeah – shuttles and satellites and that, but they don't—'

'And probes, Ben. Robot probes. They've been to Mars, Venus, Jupiter. What's to stop some alien life-form hitching a ride on one of those, eh?'

'It's impossible, Midge. Those things don't come back. They're not designed to. If they tried, they'd burn up in the atmosphere.'

'Do you know that, Ben? For sure? Are you up with all the very latest developments in space exploration?'

'Well, no, but—'

'There y'are, then. I think it's time we paid Cansfield Farm another midnight visit, Ben.'

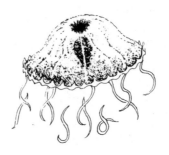

T W E N T Y - S I X

'Come here, Rex. I want to show you something.'

'What is it, Wanda?' She indicated the tank and he
followed, suppressing a shudder.

'Look.' She stood aside so he could get up close to
the observation port. She was pleased about something, he could see that.

He peered through the thick glass, cupping his
hands to cut reflection. Everything looked the same.
A mist of fine droplets issued constantly from the
ring of nozzles up around the roof, creating a perma-
nent fog which suffused what little light there was.
Through this fog the floaters moved, sluggishly and
apparently at random, like jellyfish in the cold ocean
deeps. That's exactly what they're like, he thought.
Jellyfish. Except there are no trailing tentacles and

you don't get jellyfish five metres across.

One of the creatures was passing close to the port, revolving slowly about its axis as it came. Fighting an impulse to recoil, Exley looked at it. Grey jelly. A translucent, rippling mantle of grey jelly with a great, purplish red thing pulsating at the centre like some obscene carnivorous bloom. He forced himself to examine the thing as it drifted fifteen centimetres in front of his nose, but he noticed nothing he hadn't seen before. No change. He dropped his hands and stepped back, feeling queasy.

'What am I supposed to see, Wanda?'

The woman made a clucking sound. 'The loco-motion, you great lug. The way they're moving.'

'What about it?'

'Well, can't you see? They're moving more quickly. Reacting to one another. The lethargy's going.'

He shook his head. 'They look pretty lethargic to me, sweetheart, but I'll take your word for it. What wrought the startling transformation?'

'Don't call me sweetheart, you putz.' Her hostile glance failed to conceal the triumph in her eyes. 'It's the nutrient mix. I cracked it. They're getting what they need now.'

'Good. Splendid. What is it?'

She smiled tightly. 'It wouldn't mean much to you if I told you. The thing is, it was so obvious. It was staring me right in the face the whole time and it's taken me five months to spot it.'

'What d'you mean?'

'Look – what's been our biggest problem, Rex? Apart from getting the mix right, I mean.'

'Escapes?'

'Exactly! And why were floaters escaping?'

'Well – nothing likes to be cooped up, Wanda. They just—'

'Not so! They wanted out for a reason, Rex. A particular reason. Where'd they head for, the escapers, huh? Where'd they all end up?'

'Cornfields?'

'Right! And d'you know why?'

'Not to eat corn?'

The woman laughed. 'No, but you're close. It wasn't the corn, it was something on the corn and in the earth underneath. It was a plant hormone, Rex – a modified plant hormone in a weedkiller they spray on cornfields. That same hormone, or something damn close to it, must occur in the Jovian atmosphere and it's a vital part of their diet. We've done it, Rex. They'll mature now. Breed. A few more weeks and we'll take the world by storm.'

TWENTY-SEVEN

'Straight up the track, Midge?'

'Straight up the track.'

It was two-fifteen Thursday morning. A fresh, breezy night with fast-moving cloud and intermittent moonlight. They'd met at the usual place and walked quickly along the Warminster Road, crouching in the ditch at one point while a truck went by. Now they stood at the gateway to Cansfield Farm. The roof of the house gleamed dully when the moon appeared, but the windows were dark. All was quiet, except for the shush and rattle of wind in the hedge. Ben swallowed hard and started up the track.

Alien life-forms. The phrase kept repeating inside his skull and his mind made pictures of slimy, writhing things, ill-defined but possessing many legs or tentacles. He was definitely more scared this time than last, and was appalled to realize the power Midge had over him. If anybody else had invited him to search Dan Cansfield's place for alien life-forms in the middle of the night he'd have told them to take a running jump. There was a book at home. *Any Old Place With You* it was called. It belonged to his parents and he'd never even flipped through it, but the title described his position exactly. Any old place with Midge.

Nearing the house, they paused to look and listen. The worst bit – the dark, narrow pathway between house and outbuildings – lay ahead. Nothing moved in the gloom, but a bit of loose tin roof creaked and rattled in the wind, setting Ben's nerves on edge.

He put his lips to Midge's ear. 'Do we check all these sheds and things again?'

Midge shook her head. 'No. I reckon the likeliest place is that big barn we were making for when you saw the ghost.'

They were almost clear of the house when a dog started barking somewhere inside. The pair froze, looking at each other. 'It's Bracken,' hissed Ben. 'He'll have everybody up. We'd better go back, Midge.'

'No.' Midge shook her head. 'He's barking 'cause he can hear us. He'll stop when we're past. Come on.'

They hurried on, watching the windows. No light came on, and as soon as they were clear of the house the barking stopped.

'There y'are,' whispered Midge.

'Smartie-pants,' hissed Ben. If either of them had turned at that moment, they might have seen the dim outline of a figure which flitted from shadow to shadow across the narrow path. But neither of them did.

The moon came out as they crossed the scrubby pasture. It shone on the roof of the goose-house and Midge jabbed a finger at the building. 'I bet that's where our ghost hangs out,' she whispered.

The barn doors were closed and padlocked. 'What do we do now?' said Ben. He half hoped she'd say they should go home, but she didn't.

'We'll go round,' she said. 'There might be another way in.'

They crept along the side of the building, wading through long grass and weeds. Midge had a torch with her, but they daren't show a light so close to the farm. Presently Ben said, 'Look,' and pointed. A rough opening had been cut in the barn's planking, halfway up the wall. A wooden hay chute ran down at a forty-five-degree angle from doorway to ground.

'That'll do,' grinned Midge.

Ben shivered. 'It's all right for you,' he grumbled. 'You're used to doing weird stuff in the middle of the night. I'm not.'

'I'll go first then. You keep watch.'

She stepped on to the chute and bent forward, gripping the shallow sides with both hands and inching upwards. The wood was polished from long use and the climb was far from easy, even in trainers. Ben, fóllowing the girl's ascent with his eyes, failed to see the bluish glint of moonlight along the barrel of a shotgun as its bearer merged with the barn's deep shadow.

'OK.' Midge had reached the top. Framed in the doorway, she signalled to Ben to follow.

He copied her technique and joined her, standing in almost total darkness on the creaking boards of what had to be a loft. They daren't move about because they were obviously quite high above the floor of the barn, and somewhere nearby the platform they were standing on would end in a long drop.

'Hang on,' whispered Midge. 'I'll get the torch out.' She switched on, keeping the beam low down till she located the edge of the loft, then moving it along the rim till it revealed the top of a ladder. They went over to it and Midge shone the torch down into the dark well of the barn.

'Wait,' hissed Ben, as she moved the light about. 'Go back a bit. There. What's that?' The beam reflected off something metallic.

'A van or something,' said Midge. She let the light creep slowly along the bright surface.

'Heck of a big van,' whispered Ben.

'Well, there's one end of it,' murmured Midge. 'I'll try the other way.'

She did so, tracking right along what looked like a gleaming curve. The disc of light seemed to travel a long way before the reflective surface ended. When it did, Midge back-tracked again then let the beam travel upwards, and they saw that the great metallic structure reared way above the loft, its top almost touching the beams which supported the roof.

'Wow!' gasped Midge. 'The thing's nearly as wide as the barn and nearly as high too. You know what it is, don't you, Ben?'

Ben shrugged. 'Slurry tank?'

Midge snorted. 'Why would they hide a slurry tank in a barn, Ben? No, I think we've found what we're looking for.'

'You mean that thing's an alien life-form?' Ben croaked.

'No, you div! It's a sort of tank, but I wouldn't be surprised to find alien life-forms inside it.'

'Ah.'

'Well, they'd have to be in something, wouldn't they, if their atmosphere's different? I reckon they're in there, and I'm off down to look.'

Ben knelt by the ladder, illuminating the rungs while she descended. It seemed a long way down. Presently, he saw her face upturned. 'I'm down,' she hissed. 'Come on.'

He clambered down gingerly, the torch clamped in his teeth. As soon as his feet touched the floor Midge said, 'Gimme the torch.'

Ben took it from his mouth, wiped it on his sleeve and handed it to her. 'What you gonna do?'

'Have a look in, of course.' She moved towards the tank, playing the torch about its surface till she located a window. Ben stood with one hand on the ladder, watching her, hoping it would turn out to be slurry after all. He didn't fancy being a few centimetres away from a bunch of aliens when the only way out was up a ladder and down a chute. As Midge reached the window, he thought he heard something in the blackness above. A footfall.

'Midge!' His sharp whisper echoed in the great barn. She turned. 'What is it, Ben?'

'I thought I heard something. I think there's someone in the loft.'

The torch went up, its beam sweeping the platform. 'Is there heck. Don't you want to see?' She hadn't realized he wasn't following her.

'Yes, sure.' He crossed the boards reluctantly as Midge went on tiptoe, peering through the glass.

'Wow!' Her exclamation almost stopped his heart. 'Get a look at these guys, Ben.'

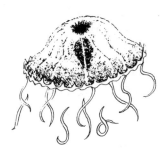

TWENTY-EIGHT

Barry sat in the loft, his back against the wall, the shotgun cradled in his arms. Except for the faint torchlight from below, he was in total darkness. He'd positioned himself well back from the edge, but from where he sat he could see the disc of light skittering across the skin of the tank and the two figures, dwarfed by the great container, moving about.

He could easily have shot them. He'd followed them up the chute and watched them negotiate the ladder. Or he could have captured them at gunpoint and handed them over to Exley. He hadn't, because he didn't want to. He'd had enough of being picked on and threatened, of being used by Free and Exley as though he was their servant. Things had been bad enough before they came, but at least he hadn't had to watch his every word like he had to now, and he'd been able to spend his nights in his bed instead of lugging this great heavy gun around the farm. Once Ben and Midge saw what was in that tank, they'd do what he daren't do himself – they'd tell the police. That'd bring the whole thing to an end, wouldn't it?

Presently, Ben and Midge turned and he watched the circle of light jerking across the boards as they returned to the ladder. At its foot they were out of his line of vision and it was almost completely dark. He listened. Voices whispered, then came the soft thud of trainers on rungs and streaks of light on the ladder's trembling shafts.

The first climber reached the top, stepped on to the platform and turned. 'Go on then, Ben,' murmured Barry. 'You've seen. Now tell the fuzz.' He listened. The girl was coming up. He knew by the erratic swing of the beam that she had the torch in her teeth. He smiled. 'Come on, Midge. You might have to push your boyfriend 'cause he's a bit of a pillock, but he'll go to the cops if you tell him to.'

The torch bobbed into view over the platform's rim. Just for fun, Barry raised the gun, tucked its butt into his shoulder and sighted along the barrel. 'This is it, Midge Fixby,' he breathed. 'Can't possibly miss you from 'ere. BANG!'

He smiled and lowered the gun as the two youngsters, totally unaware of his presence, followed the puddle of torchlight towards the chute.

★

He didn't follow when they'd gone down the chute. He sat hugging his knees in the warm darkness, listening to the wind.

They're OK, he told himself. They'll be down the track by now, and in the morning they'll tell the police what they've seen and then it'll be over. They'll take Exley and Free and those monsters away and the tank'll be dismantled and I'll be able to come up here whenever I want, like I used to before.

It was his favourite place, this loft. It was where he came when things got really bad. When his parents fought or his father was in a temper or he'd been punished. He'd sat here for hours on end, planning to run away or set fire to the house; plotting how he'd pay his father back as soon as he was big enough. The barn was in the wrong place and had long since fallen into disuse, so nobody else came here. Or they hadn't till Free and Exley showed up. They'd taken it over, hauling sections of the tank and other stuff in by night, setting it all up in the space of a few days during which he wasn't allowed near. And when it was done, his father had told his mother and himself to stay away from the barn. It was part of the deal, he said. He hadn't told Barry anything else about the agreement, except that Free and Exley were paying what he called big money, and that nobody had better muck it up for him by shooting their mouths off or snooping.

And that was that. Both Barry and his mother were frightened of Dan Cansfield so that, although the barn had remained unfastened until recently, neither of them had gone anywhere near it till last Sunday night when Barry, doing guard duty for the first time, had crept in and seen the aliens. He'd heard his father muttering about livestock, and curiosity had overcome fear.

He smiled now in the dark, picturing Free and Exley snoring in their beds while a couple of kids slipped away with their secret. ' 'T ain't a secret no more, is it?' he murmured. 'And I got you back, didn't I, just like I said I would.'

TWENTY-NINE

There hadn't been time to talk. They'd crept into Little Pitney as dawn was breaking and had gone straight home. 'We'll meet before school,' Midge had said, 'and decide what to do.'

Ben hadn't slept much. He'd lain on his back with his eyes closed and his hands clasped behind his head while aliens floated about in his skull. Now he slumped at the breakfast table, gazing into his cornflakes with hot, gritty eyes. It was ten to eight, he was meeting Midge at ten past, and his mother was giving him funny looks.

'Are you feeling unwell, Ben? You look pretty ghastly to me.'

'I'm OK, Mum. Didn't sleep too well, I don't know why.'

'I do.' His mother smiled so knowingly that he felt a pang of alarm which her next words dispelled. 'You're excited about the holidays, aren't you? Six whole weeks in which to do exactly as you please.' She laughed. 'I'd be excited.' The library didn't close for the summer and his mother got only a fortnight.

'No, you wouldn't,' said her husband, who'd be getting six weeks also. 'Not if you had to spend it decorating, as I do.' Ben's father always felt vaguely guilty about getting three times as much holiday as his wife, and he dealt with his guilt by painting the outside of the house and tinkering with the car.

'You don't have to paint every summer,' his wife replied. 'Every second year would be quite sufficient in my opinion, but still.'

Ben laid down his spoon and pushed back his chair, thankful that his parents' bickering had diverted their attention from himself. He stood up. His father was going on about the necessity of maintaining one's property. Nobody noticed Ben's uneaten breakfast. Nobody called him back.

Midge was leaning on the phone-box outside Tarkington's. There were no other kids about yet. It was too early.

'Hi, Midge.'

'Hi, Ben. Sleep OK?'

'No.'

'Me neither. I was thinking what to do.'

'So, what do we do?'

She shook her head. 'I don't know. I thought we'd be telling the police, but I don't think we can.'

'Why not?'

'Well, would they be interested, Ben? Are any laws being broken up at Cansfield?'

'What?' Ben looked at her. 'Keeping things from outer space in secret on a farm? You can't do that, can you?'

Midge shrugged. 'I bet there's no law against it, 'cause nobody ever did it before. And anyway, Ken Aspinall wouldn't believe us, would he? He'd think we were winding him up.'

'Why is it such a big secret then, if it's not against the law?'

'I don't know, do I? Could be all sorts of reasons, Ben.'

'Well, how about telling the papers? They'd be interested. They've been full of stuff about corn circles and there's got to be a connection.'

'What connection, Ben? How does a tankful of giant jellyfish cause corn circles?'

'Well—' Ben shook his head. 'I dunno, Midge, but there's got to be a connection, hasn't there? It'd be a fantastic coincidence if Cansfield had aliens and corn circles at the same time and there was no connection. Maybe they get out.'

'Who?'

'The aliens. Perhaps they get out of the tank.'

'Shouldn't think so, Ben. Our atmosphere'd kill 'em, wouldn't it? That's why they have to live in a tank.'

'Hmm. Well, I reckon we should tell the papers.'

'Will they believe us though?'

'That friend of yours – Mrs Tattersall. Couldn't we try her?'

Midge pulled a face. 'We could, I suppose, but she's not a reporter, she's a librarian.'

'She knows some reporters though, doesn't she? The guy on the *Guardian*?'

'Yes, but we'd have to get her to believe us before she'd tell anybody else, and that won't be easy.'

'Can we try though, Midge – this afternoon?'

Midge shrugged. 'OK. We'll give it a try. Meet me here at quarter to four and I'll give her a ring.'

At breaktime, Ben was one of a group of volunteers getting the hall ready for the leavers' disco, so Midge was alone on the field when Barry approached her.

'How d'you like your auntie's pets?' he asked.

Midge frowned. 'What?'

'Your auntie's pets. Floaters, she calls them. I heard her talking to the queer feller about 'em. How d'you like 'em?'

'I don't know what you're talking about, Barry.' She was beginning to though, and her heart speeded up.

'Oh, come on! Auntie Wanda, remember? The one you told me about? You saw her on our track.'

'She's not my auntie.'

'No, I know. You made a pillock out of me, Midge.' He gazed at her. 'I could've blown your head off in our barn at two this morning but I let you get away. You and him. Have you told the police?'

Midge shook her head. 'No.' She felt sick. 'You mean you were there? You saw us?'

'How else would I know you were there? I had my dad's gun. You had a flashlight in your teeth, and I could've blown you away but I wanted you to get the fuzz.'

'We can't, Barry. Nobody's breaking the law, and anyway they wouldn't believe me.'

'You could try 'em, Midge. I want it stopped, what's going on up home.'

'Why don't you tell them, then?'

'You're joking! They'd tell my dad I split on him and he'd murder me. It's gotta be someone else, Midge.'

Midge nodded. 'Ben reckons the papers might be interested, so we're ringing somebody this aft. A friend of my parents. Trouble is, she probably won't believe us.' She looked at him. 'She'd be more likely to believe you, Barry.'

'Oh no!' Barry shook his head. 'No way, Midge. Not a chance. I told you, he'd murder me.'

'Tell me something, then.'

'What?'

'Do Wanda's pets have anything to do with corn circles?'

'Oh, ah. They make 'em.'

'How?'

'They escape, see. Float away, land in the field, flatten the corn.'

'How d'you know, Barry?'

'Her voice carries, see. She has these rows with Exley and you can hear every word.'

'But the corn's so tidy, y'know? It all lies one way and none of the stalks is broken and the edges are really sharp. It doesn't look as though it's been squashed by a giant jellyfish.'

Barry shrugged. 'I don't know how it's done 'cause I never seen it, but it's floaters all right. And after they done it, they melt.'

'Melt?'

'Ah. Too warm for 'em, see? Cold where they come from.'

'Where's that?'

'Dunno. Nobody talks about that. Big secret.'

Midge pulled a face. 'Well, we'll have to see what happens with this friend of my parents. Maybe it'll all come out and they'll put a stop to it.'

Barry nodded. 'Let me know then. Tomorrow. And keep my name out of it. OK?'

'Mrs Tattersall?'

'Speaking.'

'Oh, it's Midge again, Mrs Tattersall. Midge Fixby. Can I ask you something?'

'Of course.'

'Well – suppose you'd found something out – something really interesting and unusual – and you wanted to get it in the papers, what would you do?'

'If it was me, Midge, I'd phone the newsdesk and tell them all about it.'

'And they'd send somebody out?'

'If they were sufficiently interested, yes. Why – have you got something interesting?'

'Yes. You know corn circles?'

'I know of them, Midge.'

'And you know what you told us about Wanda Free and Rex Exley?'

'Ye-es.'

'Well, we know what causes corn circles and it's something absolutely fantastic and we don't know if anyone'll believe us.'

'Just a minute, Midge. Where do Exley and Free fit into this? You told me you were doing something for school.'

'No, I just said it was a scientific investigation. It's something Ben and I are doing on our own.'

'Ah. And are you going to tell me about your fantastic discovery, Midge?'

'If I do, will you pass it on to your friend at the *Guardian*?'

'That rather depends, Midge. I can't promise till I've heard your story.'

'No.' Midge pulled a face at Ben, who had crammed himself into the box with her and was trying to listen in. 'Well, what it is, Mrs Tattersall, it's these things from outer space. They're like giant jellyfish and they float in the air and Free and Exley have got them in a tank up Cansfield Farm.'

There was a brief silence. When the woman spoke again her tone had cooled. 'Are you making fun of me, Midge? I heard somebody giggle.'

'No, I'm not, Mrs Tattersall, honestly. Ben laughed 'cause it sounds so ridiculous, but it's true. We've seen them.'

'How?'

'Pardon?'

'How have you seen them? Are you telling me these creatures are on open display somewhere?'

'Oh no. They're hidden in a barn. A locked barn. We went there last night, very late. Barry – that's Dan Cansfield's son – was guarding them with a gun but he let us go 'cause he wanted us to tell the police.'

'And have you?' Ben thrust his face at hers, mouthing, 'Liar.'

She shoved him away. 'No, we haven't, Mrs Tattersall.'

'Why not?'

'Well, they'd never believe us, would they?'

'No, Midge, I don't think they would, and I'm sorry, but neither do I. It's totally preposterous. I don't know what sort of game you're playing, you and your friend, but I can tell you I'm not at all amused. In fact, I've a good mind to speak to your parents about it.'

'But it's true, Mrs Tattersall – every word. How can I make you believe me?'

'Now that's enough, Midge, d'you hear? I have work to do. I'm going to hang up and, if you persist in this silly prank, your parents will come to hear of it. Goodbye.'

The second they left the box, Ben grabbed her sleeve. 'Why'd you give her all that stuff about Barry, Midge? Maybe she'd have listened if you hadn't lied.'

'Get off me!' She knocked his hand away. 'It wasn't a lie, Ben. Barry was there. He could've blown our heads off.'

Ben's cheeks paled. 'You're putting me on, right?'

Midge shook her head. Ben swallowed. 'So he's on our side?' The notion of Barry Cansfield as a friend and ally wasn't easy to take.

Midge nodded. 'We'd be dead if he wasn't.'

'Hmm. So what do we do, Midge – tell somebody else?'

'No point. We need proof, Ben. Photos.'

'Photos?'

'Sure, why not? Barry might help.'

'When – tonight?'

'No. School finishes tomorrow, right? We might as well wait a day or two and do it in the hols when we can sleep late after.'

Ben grinned. 'You're a genius, Midge. You think of everything.'

Midge gave her Mona Lisa smile. 'Somebody's got to,' she said.

THIRTY

Everything had been cleared away so you couldn't
tell there'd been a disco, but school felt different that
Friday morning. There was that delicious winding-
down, stalling-along feeling you always get on the
last day before the holidays – the sense that nothing
very serious is going to be attempted by even the
keenest teacher – that in a way the holidays have
already started.

There were no fights. No hassles. Everybody seemed
cheerful except some of the leavers who drifted around,
pasty-faced and dreamy, waiting for emotion to over-
whelm them.

At morning break, Ben found Midge sitting on the
grass in a far corner of the playing field. 'Four hours
to go,' he said.

She looked up smiling, shielding screwed-up eyes. 'Yeah. Wonder what it feels like, leaving.'

'Us next year, Midge.'

'Yeah. Find out then, won't we? Will you cry, d'you think?'

'No chance. You?'

'Dunno. Everybody says they won't, but some always do. Can't tell till the time comes, I reckon.'

'Pitney Prim.' Ben laughed. 'Can't imagine missing it myself.' He squinted across the field towards the cluster of low buildings he'd first entered a million years ago, when he was five. 'Pitney Prim, Pitney Prim, the teachers are crazy and the kids are dim.' The school rap. Unofficial, of course, but quite old and the teachers knew about it.

'The teachers are crazy,' amended Midge, 'and some of the kids are dim.'

'OK, OK.' Ben gazed at her, hoping they'd still be friends at the big school in Trowbridge. 'It wasn't composed with you in mind, Einstein.'

Barry came shambling up just before the bell, looking anxious. 'What happened with that friend of yours – the papers?'

Midge told him and he said, 'So what happens now? You leaving it or what?'

She shook her head. 'We're not leaving it, and we might need your help. How do we get you in the hols?'

Barry shrugged. 'I'll be around. Don't come up home, and don't phone or you'll get me killed. There's always Koffee Korner, Saturdays.'

'And in between?'

He shrugged again. 'Anywhere, when he lets me off. The woods. Here. Tarkington's. You know.'

Midge nodded. 'We'll see you, then.'

'Yeah.' He lingered, hands in pockets, hacking turf with a boot toe. 'Don't just leave it, eh?'

'No,' said Midge. 'I told you.'

The bell went.

THIRTY-ONE

It was eight o'clock Saturday morning, and at Cansfield Farm breakfast was over. Dan and Barry had gone off to fix a broken gate. Frieda was clearing the table. Wanda Free and Rex Exley sat glowering at each other across the board as plates, mugs and cutlery were whipped away. They were arguing.

'It's ridiculous,' grumbled Exley, hoovering up toast crumbs with a fingertip and sprinkling them into a saucer. 'Every day that passes – every hour – increases the danger of exposure, yet you insist on continuing to observe, as you call it. Waiting for something to happen. Baby floaters or whatever. And if you get them, you'll want to wait till one of them dies so you'll know how long they live. Don't you see, we could be here forever at this rate?'

Free's hand sketched a dismissive gesture. 'You're not a scientist, Rex. You don't understand. All you care about's the money. The fame. I want those things too, but most of all I want to learn. I want to know all there is to know about these creatures. It's a dream, this chance I've got, and I'm not about to drop it just because a bunch of hick-town kids're getting curious.'

'It may be kids now,' retorted Exley, 'but kids talk, and if they suspect something – if they have so much as an inkling of what we've got here – it's only a matter of time until some nosy parent or teacher gets to hear about it and goes to the authorities. The minute that happens, your friends at NASA will descend on this place like the proverbial ton of bricks. It was you who told me their policy on alien life-forms – that none must be brought to Earth or even into the atmosphere, for fear they might carry bacteria or viruses which could wipe out terrestrial life. Those guys'll destroy everything, Wanda, everything, and the two of us could find ourselves in jail.'

Frieda Cansfield coughed apologetically. ' 'Scuse me, but if you've finished in here, I ought to make a start on my cleaning.'

'Yes, of course, Mrs Cansfield.' Exley pushed back his chair, stood up and leaned across the table. 'Wanda,' he said, quietly. 'If those pets of yours are showing no change a week from today, I'm going public and you can go hang.'

'Rex.' The woman's voice was cold. 'It so happens that those pets of mine are showing change right now.'

120

She rose and, coming round the table, took him by the arm and began steering him from the room. 'I know you hate to look at the floaters but I'm gonna show you anyway, and I'm gonna tell you something too.' She tightened her grip on his arm and dropped her voice to an icy hiss.

'You go public, Rex, or you breathe a single word to anyone about my work, and I swear I'll kill you.'

As Free and Exley were approaching the barn, the phone rang at Ben's house. Ben was dozing in bed when his mother called up the stairs. 'Ben – are you awake?'

'Uh-huh.' He rolled over, yawning. 'What's up?' It was Saturday and the first day of the hols. Why was Mum getting him up?'

'Phone for you. A young woman.'

Young woman? He groaned and sat up, running a quick check on young women who might phone him. There were none. He swung his legs out of bed. 'Who is it, Mum?'

'It's Midge, dear. Are you coming?'

Midge. Why the heck hadn't she said so? 'Yes, I'm coming.' He slid his feet into his slippers, rushed downstairs and grabbed the receiver. 'Hello, Midge?'

'Hi, Ben. Guess what?'

'Uh – you grew another head in the night?'

'Idiot.'

'Best I can do this time of morning, so I give up. What is it?'

'My folks've only sprung a trip on me, that's all. We leave in an hour.'

'What sort of trip? Where?'

'Scotland. Part-business, part-pleasure, Dad says. Somebody's selling a restaurant near a place called Banff and he wants to look at it. We'll be gone a week.'

Ben's heart kicked. 'A restaurant in Scotland? Does that mean—?'

'I don't know what it means, Ben. They don't talk to me. Anyway, we'll have to leave that little matter we discussed till the week after. What'll you do?'

'Oh, mess around in general, I suppose. I certainly won't go near Cansfield.' He pulled a face. 'Maybe I'll sit in the bus shelter at two in the morning and think about you.' As soon as he said this he got an aching lump in his throat and said, thickly, 'Hey, Midge – don't let 'em buy it. Don't move to Scotland, hey?'

Midge sighed. 'It's not up to me, is it? I don't want to go away, even for a week, but kids go where their folks go, right?'

'Right.' He inhaled deeply, fighting the lump. 'So have a nice time and I'll call you a week from today. What time?'

'Better make it Sunday, Ben. We're back Saturday but it'll probably be late. You take care now.'

'Yeah, you too. 'Bye.' He listened for the click then hung up, knuckled the wet from his eyes and went upstairs to get dressed.

T H I R T Y - T W O

Exley peered through the fogged glass, watching with distaste the apparently aimless, drifting motion of the floaters. Behind him, Wanda Free awaited his reaction. 'Well?'

Exley shrugged. 'Can't see anything new, Wanda. Never can with these things.'

The woman sighed. 'Single one out. One of the bigger ones. Look at the edge of the mantle.' She waited, biting her lower lip.

Exley nodded. 'I'm looking.'

'Well – what d'you notice?'

'Er – bumps? Sort of swellings, all round the edge?'

'Right. Now the swellings aren't very advanced on the individual you've chosen, but if you look around you'll see that on some of them those bumps, as you

123

call them, have become more pronounced. They're cone-like. They come to a point.'

'Ah, yes. I see one. What does it mean, Wanda?'

'I dunno, Rex. It could be anything. Maturity. Pregnancy. Ageing. It's a matter of waiting to see what happens next.'

Exley turned to look at her. 'It always is, Wanda. That's the trouble.' He saw the light in her eyes, the dangerous light, and changed the subject. 'Why do they rotate all the time?'

'Sensors. They have sensors all round the rim of the mantle. It's how they locate their food, each other, whatever. Rotation gives 'em a fix, y'know – distance, direction?'

He grimaced. 'Too deep for me, I'm afraid. So, how long, d'you think?'

She gazed at him, levelly. 'As long as it takes,' she said.

T H I R T Y - T H R E E

It was a fairly boring week for Ben. The weather wasn't all that good and he'd probably have sat at home reading most of the time, but his dad started painting the outside of the house and Ben had to disappear or he'd have been roped in to assist. He hung around the Village Hall, where Wayne Daykin and some of the other kids played pool or table tennis and used the game machines. When he tired of that, he wandered off to walk alone in Pitney Wood or through the narrow lanes. He didn't see Barry, and guessed the poor prannock was helping get the crops in. Some dads you can dodge, but Dan Cansfield wasn't one of them.

On Thursday there was a postcard from Midge, with a view of Inverness. On the back she'd written:

'Cool, windy, beautiful but naff-all to do. Roll on Sunday. Midge.' It cheered him up a bit because it meant she was thinking of him, but he wished she'd signed it love from, and of course it did nothing to ease his worry over that rotten restaurant.

The week passed like a thousand years. Saturday he woke up feeling good, and at lunchtime he volunteered to paint the garden gate so he could keep an eye on the road. It was a warm day at the height of the tourist season and, during the course of the afternoon, hundreds of cars went by, but the Fixby Saab wasn't among them. He took his time over the paint job, but by five o'clock it was done. He cleaned up, gobbled a sandwich and spent the long evening strolling up and down High Street. When it got to ten o'clock and they still hadn't come, he plonked himself on the bench in the bus shelter and chatted with a middle-aged couple who gave him a funny look when they got on the last bus and he didn't.

It was twenty-five to eleven when the Saab went by. It was pretty dark, but he saw Midge in the back and she seemed to peer at the shelter as the vehicle slowed to make the right-hand turn into Tansy Road. He waved, but couldn't tell if she saw.

'Where've you been, Ben?' asked his father when he walked into the house. 'It's twenty to eleven and your mother's been worried sick.'

'Sorry,' mumbled Ben. 'I was only sitting in the bus shelter.'

'Till half-past ten at night?'

Yes, he thought. And at two and three and four in the morning, but he didn't say it. Instead he said, 'I was watching the traffic and lost track of time. I didn't mean to worry you, Mum.'

'That's all right, dear,' said his mother. She smiled. 'It's a very long drive from Scotland.'

T H I R T Y - F O U R

It was night when the real change came. The terrestrials slept. There was no witness.

During the course of the evening the largest floater had risen till it hung just beneath the domed roof of the tank. Spikes like a crown of thorns circled its mantle. It had ceased to rotate. Instead, it began a sort of bobbing motion: ascending a little, sinking back, ascending again, like a boat on an oily swell. As it did so, a shallow depression appeared at the centre of its mantle. Gradually this deepened, so that the creature appeared to be falling into itself. As the hollow deepened, a bump appeared on the floater's underside, growing as the depression on top became more pronounced. As the process continued, the spiked rim of the floater's mantle was drawn in towards the centre and the creature's diameter slowly shrank as it poured its substance into the bump which hung from its underside, elongating like a great glob of wax falling in slow motion from a melting candle. For a while the creature resembled a monstrous, floating flower, its ring of spiky petals closing. But as the process of change became complete, an observer would have realized that the flower's head had become a great mouth ringed with spiky teeth: that the floater, by turning itself inside out, had become another creature.

THIRTY-FIVE

The day Ben got the card from Midge, Wanda Free began acting strangely. She had Dan Cansfield move her bed out of the goose-house and set it up in the tiny glass and plastic cubicle inside the barn. When he'd done this, she took him round the side of the building and pointed to the hay chute. 'That thing,' she said. 'Get rid of it.'

Dan Cansfield wasn't accustomed to being ordered around. He thought seriously about smacking Wanda Free across the head, but then he remembered the money she and Exley were paying him and did as he was told.

When she'd seen the chute removed, Wanda went up to the house and handed the farmer's wife a shopping list. Frieda glanced at the list, then looked at the scientist and stammered, 'I'm sorry, Miss Free, I don't mean to question your wishes, but you've written ten pounds of—'

'I know what I've written, Mrs Cansfield.'

'But what will you do with it all?'

'Don't you worry about that, Mrs Cansfield, that's my affair. Could you leave right away, please – I'd like that stuff by noon.'

Rex Exley watched these events with anxiety. He'd spotted his partner's strangeness the first time they'd met, but in the last few days he'd noticed a marked deterioration in her behaviour and appearance. Her face had thinned, the waxy skin drawn tight over bone. Her dark eyes seemed large and unnaturally bright. They shifted constantly and bore a haunted look. Wanda had grown so jumpy and furtive she reminded him of a timid small creature that wants only to scurry away into the dark, but which will fight fiercely if cornered.

He fell in beside her as she left the house. 'How are the pets?' he asked lightly. 'Coming along?'

'They're fine.'

'All spiky round the edges, I suppose?'

'Uh-huh.'

'Anything else?'

'Whaddya mean, anything else?'

There was something, then. He faked a rueful smile. 'No need to bite my head off, old girl. What I mean is, has anyone laid an egg, changed colour, died?'

'No.'

'Nothing for me to look at, then?'

'Nothing.'

'You've moved in with them, I see. Why's that?'

'Security. I've no confidence in your arrangements, Rex. You don't check up on your guards.'

'Oh thanks, Wanda. That's charming. I need my sleep too, y'know.'

'Yeah well, you'll get it now. I'm watching 'em myself.'

'The guards?'

'Guards, floaters, the lot.'

'What about sleep, Wanda? You don't want to crack up.'

'Crack up?' She laughed, a brief shrill laugh. 'I'm not gonna crack up.' They were approaching the barn. 'Have you nothing to do, Rex?'

'Plenty, thanks. I thought I'd pop in and peep at the pets first, that's all.'

'No, Rex, please. Not now. My work's entering a crucial phase. I don't want them disturbed.'

'OK.' He forced the smile again. 'Never let it be said that Rex Exley inflicted himself where he wasn't wanted. I'll see you at dinner.'

He left her, thinking, something's going on. Something she doesn't want me to know about. I'll bide my time and, when she's not looking, I'll slip in there and have a quick shufti.

THIRTY - SIX

He didn't feel like phoning her from home. His mother had embarrassed him last night with her remark about the long drive from Scotland. Parents who'll make cracks like that might listen when you're on the phone. He told his mother he didn't fancy breakfast and went across to the box outside Tarkington's.

'Hello? Oh hi, Mr Fixby. It's Ben Lockwood. Could I speak to Midge, please? Thanks.' He waited. A fat man in sandals went by with a little white poodle on a lead.

'Hi, Ben.'

'Midge. Welcome back. Did I get you up?'

'No, I've been up ages.'

'Show-off. Thanks for the card, by the way. Did you see me last night?'

'Where?'

'In the shelter. I waved.'

'No, sorry.'

'It doesn't matter. Did you have fun?'

'Not really. There's some fantastic scenery and the people're nice, but they seem to get a lot of rain.'

'Ah-ha. What happened about the restaurant?'

'Dunno. We went there and the guy showed them round. I stayed outside and sulked so they'd know I wasn't keen. When we drove past the place in the evening, there weren't many cars in the car park, and the nearest school's eleven miles away. I don't think they were too impressed, actually.'

'Good.' He felt better, too. A surge of relief. 'Can you come out?'

'We're finishing breakfast. Half an hour?'

'Sure. Where?'

'Guess.'

He left the booth and sauntered along High Street with his hands in his pockets, whistling. It was the sort of bright morning that promises a hot day to come. The fat man, heading back, nodded. 'Morning.'

'Morning,' went Ben, and the poodle sniffed his trainer as it passed.

He had the shelter to himself. It was ten to nine and there'd be no bus till eleven. There were two empty beer bottles on the bench, and Ben remembered his grandad telling him how when he was a kid, they used to go round finding empties because you got a penny each for them at the offie. A penny. They must've been poor in those days.

Midge appeared at quarter past. He wanted to hug her but grinned instead and said, 'Bang on time.' He put the bottles under the bench so she could sit down. She smiled. 'Boozing, eh?'

'Oh, ah. Nothin' like a coupla pints after breakfast, my dear. Good for the innards.'

'Don't be disgusting. What shall we do?'

Ben shrugged. 'Sit here. Or we could go up the wood if you like.'

'Let's do that, then. You can tell me what you've been up to all week.'

They strolled back through the village, and as Ben was showing off his paint job on the gate his mother appeared in the window. He didn't look at her but his cheeks burned and he knew he was blushing. 'Come on, Midge,' he muttered.

They walked on, turning left into Grange Lane. The width of the road separated the row of cottages, which included Ben's house, from the churchyard. Worshippers tended to use the lane as a car park, and a line of vehicles now stretched from the end of the lane almost to the gateway of Pitney Grange, a distance of nearly a quarter of a mile.

'Looks like a full house for Mr Cribb this morning, Midge.'

'Does, doesn't it? What if the Grange caught fire

during the service? They'd never get a fire engine past this lot.'

'No way. Do you ever go to church, Midge?'

'No. Sunday's a working day for my folks. They sent me to Sunday School when I was little, though.'

'I used to come to Sunday School. I don't remember seeing you.'

'Not here, you div. We didn't live here then.'

'Where did you live?'

'Wootton Bassett. It's near Swindon. We had a restaurant. I was born there.'

'In a restaurant?'

'Upstairs, stupid. We lived above the business. Moved here when I was seven.'

'Ah.'

They passed the last of the parked vehicles and paused to gaze in through the wide gateway of Pitney Grange. It was a big old house with a balustraded terrace and many windows. Once it had belonged to the local squires, but it was Major Fairbairn's now. The Major was retired from the Army, and he and his wife were governors of Pitney Prim.

'When I was a little kid,' said Ben, 'I thought Dracula lived here. Me and my mates used to run past this gateway, especially if it was getting dark.'

Midge nodded. 'I can imagine. You'd run now if I wasn't here to protect you.'

'Cheek!' He took a playful swipe at her head which she easily dodged, and they moved on. As they did so, there was a volley of barking and a shaggy old spaniel came bounding towards them.

'It's Rudge!' cried Ben. 'C'mon, Rudge. Here, boy!' The dog reared, planted its forepaws on Ben's chest and began licking his cheeks, wagging its tail frantically as the boy slapped its neck and ruffled its loppy ears. After a few seconds he pushed the animal away, laughing. 'Geroff, Rudge, you messy beast. Go slobber on Midge for a change.'

'Don't you dare!' Midge made shooing motions with her arms and Rudge swerved away, barking excitedly.

Rudge was the Major's dog. It was older than Ben, and had known the boy since he was a toddler. As he and Midge continued towards the wood the dog followed, running circles round them in the hope of getting a game. Ben stopped and waved it away. 'Go home now, Rudge, there's a good dog. Go on, boy.' He was fond of the animal, but a quiet stroll with Midge seemed most unlikely with Rudge around. The dog ignored him, circling the couple twice before racing on ahead.

As it passed between the first trees, Grange Lane dwindled to a footpath which meandered through the wood and beyond, leading eventually to the village of Corsley Heath. It was seldom trodden by tourists, and this made it a popular walk with local people. It was still quite early though and, as Midge and Ben entered the wood, it seemed they had it to themselves.

It was a bright, still morning. The sun, glimpsed as a dazzle through foliage, cast a lattice of shadow on the dusty path. Myriad insects danced in the greenish light, their noise palpable in the intervals between sprays of bird-song, and the air was fragrant with a scent compounded of fungi, flowers and sweet rottenness. As they sauntered, Ben reached for the girl's cool, bony hand, wrapping his warm hand round it. She gave him a sidelong glance but let the hand remain, murmuring, 'Lovely, isn't it?'

'Mmm.' There was a crashing in the undergrowth and the dog lolloped across the path in front of them, its long tongue lolling, and disappeared on the other side. 'Silly old mutt,' smiled Ben. 'He's kidding himself he's flushed out a rabbit and he couldn't even catch a tortoise, he's so old and slow.'

'Don't be rotten,' cried Midge. 'You'll be old and slow yourself someday.'

'Ah – if Dan Cansfield doesn't shoot me first.'

'Oh, Ben, what d'you say that for? I was enjoying this walk till you reminded me of all that Cansfield stuff. I was hoping we wouldn't talk about it, just for once.'

Ben squeezed her hand. 'Sorry, Midge. It was a joke. I promise I won't mention another— What the heck's that?' A drawn-out cry drowned Ben's words and drained the colour from his cheeks.

'Dunno.' Midge gulped. 'Sounded like Rudge.'

'That's what I thought.' He peered through the trees. 'Maybe he's stepped into a trap or—' There was a second shivering cry followed by a sharp yelp, then silence.

Ben had started towards the sound and, when it stopped, he paused, calling. 'Rudge? What is it boy – whatsamatter, Rudge?'

'Sssh!' Midge grabbed his sleeve. 'Listen.'

He couldn't hear anything at first. Nothing at all. The birds had stopped singing. The insects themselves seemed shocked into silence. Then, from somewhere up ahead came a viscous, snuffling noise that made him go cold. He looked at Midge. 'It sounds like something—'

The word stuck in his mouth and Midge said, 'Eating. It sounds like something eating.' The notion conjured grisly pictures in their minds but they crept towards the sound, peering into the green dimness between the trees.

They'd moved only a short distance when Midge touched Ben's shoulder and pointed. Twenty metres away, half-hidden by a clump of seedling oaks, the spaniel lay dead, its coat damp and spiky with blood. Crouched over the carcass was a creature whose appearance filled Ben with such horror that in the instant of seeing it he cried out. At the sound of his voice the creature lifted its head and grew still, returning the children's gaze with cold, reptilian eyes while ropes of its victim's gore dribbled from its spike-crammed jaws.

'Wh-what the heck is it, Midge?'

'I dunno. It's looking straight at us. Don't move.'

'Its teeth.' Ben shuddered. 'Look at its teeth. Is it some sort of snake or what?'

'No, it's got limbs.'

'D'you think if we run—?'

'It caught Rudge, Ben.'

'Well, how about backing off slowly?'

'Give it a try, I suppose, but what if it comes for us?'

'If it comes for us we run.'

'OK.'

Slowly, keeping their eyes on the creature and avoiding sudden movements, the pair began to retreat. To their inexpressible relief, the thing remained motionless, continuing to stare in their direction. When the space between it and them had grown to some fifty metres and they could no longer see the creature through the trees, Midge whispered, 'I think we're OK, Ben. If it was going to attack it'd have done it by now.'

They ran.

THIRTY - SEVEN

Len Tench was on his knees in the pink gravel drive, grubbing out a dandelion root, when Ben and Midge came pelting through the gateway of Pitney Grange. He looked up and the girl called to him. 'Mr Tench – come quick. Something awful's happened to Rudge.'

At sixty-nine, Len Tench no longer did anything quickly, and by the time he'd got to his feet the children were with him, gesturing towards the wood and jiggling in agitation.

'Now just be still a minute,' he growled, 'and tell me what happened.'

'It's Rudge,' gasped Ben. 'Something attacked him. He's dead.'

The old gardener saw tears on the boy's cheek and spoke gently.

'Dead, my dear? Now how d'you know he's dead, eh?'

'We saw him, Mr Tench. His fur's all covered in blood and this thing's eating him.'

'Eating 'im?' Tench frowned. 'What sort of critter would this be – what's he look like, boy?'

'It's a horrible thing, Mr Tench – a monster. I've never seen anything like it.'

'It's long and thin,' put in Midge, 'with fishy eyes and a great mouthful of sharp teeth. It stared at us. Have you got a gun, Mr Tench?'

The old man shook his head. 'No, missy. I got no gun.' He lifted his cap and scratched his head. 'See – there's nothing in Pitney Wood big enough to kill a dog. There's badgers and foxes and weasels – was it some kind of bird you saw?'

The children shook their heads and the gardener looked towards the house. 'I'd get the Major, only he's gone to church.' He looked at Midge. 'You'd best take me to 'im, my dear. Old Rudge, I mean.'

'You'll need something, Mr Tench – a weapon. That thing'll still be there.'

'Naw.' The old man shook his head. 'We'll holler and beat the trees with sticks. That'll see 'im off, you see if it don't.'

He was right. Approaching the spot, they picked up bits of wood and advanced slowly, whooping and yodelling and striking tree trunks till their sticks broke. Ben was dubious – he kept seeing those cold eyes, that awful mouth – but when they came in

144

sight of the victim's torn body, he saw that the creature had gone.

One close-up glance was more than enough for Ben and Midge. Sickened, they withdrew, leaving Len Tench to inspect the remains and poke about in the immediate vicinity. Ben felt nervous. The creature was probably nearby, watching them, impatient to resume its ghastly meal. He kept looking across at the old man, wondering what he was doing, wishing he'd hurry up.

When he finally joined them he said, 'Well, I don't know. It had to be something pretty big to do that to the poor old boy, but I can't find no tracks nor nothing. My guess is it was a bird – a big 'un, escaped from some zoo or somewhere. Longleat, mebbe.'

Ben shook his head. 'It was no bird, Mr Tench. It was more like – like a dragon.'

'Dragon?' The old man chuckled. 'Weren't many o' them about, even when I were a lad. Naw.' He shook his head. 'Light's none too good under trees, and you were both scairt. You seen something, and you took it for something else. Happens all the time.'

Ben didn't argue. He felt sick. They started back and Midge said, 'What will happen, Mr Tench?'

The old man shrugged. 'I'll tell the Major, first thing. He'll want to see for hisself, and then I 'spect he'll get the police. They'll ask around, see who's lost a dangerous critter.'

They left him at the gate and walked down Grange Lane. Morning service was over and the cars had gone, but they couldn't see the Major. The sun beat down so strongly the top of Ben's head stung. He looked at Midge. 'What d'you want to do?'

She shook her head. 'I think we ought to tell somebody about that monster, but who?'

'Major'll tell the police, Len said.'

'I know, and they'll be looking for a bird, won't they? A bird!' She kicked a stone at the dusty verge. 'You don't think we could've been mistaken, do you?'

'Naw.' Ben shook his head. 'Do you?'

'No.' She shivered in spite of the heat. 'Those eyes. That mouth. D'you know what it reminded me of?'

'No, what?'

'You know those fish you see pictures of – the ones that live really deep down in the ocean? It was like one of those.'

Ben nodded. 'I know what you mean. They're really ugly and you can see right through them and they have those huge mouths full of teeth. It was like one of them, except it had limbs of some sort and was much bigger. But fish don't come on land so what the heck was it?'

'I don't know, do I?' They'd reached the lane end. 'Where now?'

Ben smiled. 'Guess,' he said.

They loitered till the midday bus emptied the shelter, then moved in and occupied the bench. It was pleasantly cool, and the next bus wasn't due till one.

'D'you think the police'll want to talk to us?' asked Ben.

'Hmm.' Midge nodded. 'I hadn't thought of that, but they probably will. I mean, we were there, right? We saw the monster. We're the only witnesses. Maybe we should go home and wait.'

'If you came home with me,' Ben suggested, 'they wouldn't have to bother calling at your place.'

She smiled. 'They might try my place first.'

'Your place, then. I could phone home, tell 'em where I am. I wouldn't have eaten lunch anyway.'

'Me neither.' She shuddered. 'I don't think I'll ever eat again.'

'Will your folks mind my showing up?'

'My folks aren't there, Ben. They go to work at eleven. Listen.' She looked at him. 'The reason I didn't think of the police was, I was thinking about something else.'

'What?'

'The monster. What it is, where it came from.'

'And?'

'I think it's from Cansfield.'

'Cansfield? Why Cansfield? We didn't see anything like that when we were there.'

She nodded. 'I know. We saw giant jellyfish. They seemed soft and slow and harmless, like tadpoles.'

He stared at her. 'What you on about, Midge? What's tadpoles got to do with it?'

'Suppose they were tadpoles, Ben?'

He laughed. 'You're a nut, Midge. I knew it the minute you told me about sitting here in the middle of the night. You're totally out of your tree.'

Midge shook her head. 'No I'm not, Ben. What I'm saying is perfectly reasonable. Think about it. You've kept tadpoles. You know how it goes. Tadpoles're soft, harmless creatures. They eat plants. Nobody needs to be scared of a tadpole – not even a fly. But then they start to change and suddenly they're not tadpoles any more. They're frogs – strong, fast and carnivorous, and it's watch out mister fly.'

Ben's smile faded and he murmured, 'You mean those jellyfish might've changed into monsters? Is that what you're saying?'

She nodded. 'Why not? They're aliens, right? Nobody can possibly know their life-story – not even Wanda Free. They might have changed, and those two creepazoids up Cansfield might have got just as big a shock as we did.'

'Hmm.' Ben frowned. 'But even if you're right, Midge; if all those floaters we saw in the tank *are* monsters now, how did that one get out?'

Midge shrugged. 'Who knows? Floaters got out and made circles in the corn, didn't they?' She pulled a face. 'Anyway, I might be completely wrong. Probably am.' She stood up. 'Come on – we mustn't keep Constable Aspinall waiting.'

THIRTY-EIGHT

What Ben and Midge saw in the wood that Sunday morning, Rex Exley had seen three days earlier in the tank at Cansfield Farm. He'd slipped into the barn while Wanda was busy unloading some bulky plastic carriers from the back of Frieda Cansfield's battered Suzuki, and had counted twenty-six of the hideous beasts before his partner became aware of his presence and put an end to his counting.

'What are they?' he'd asked the furious woman. 'Where are the floaters?' Not that he'd ever liked the floaters, but they were fluffy kittens compared to what he'd seen just now.

'They are the floaters, dummy!' she'd snarled. 'I told you there'd be developments if we gave it time.'

'Developments, yes. You didn't tell me we'd end up with a tankful of dragons.' He looked at the carriers she'd stacked against the wall. 'What's in those?'

'Beef.'

'Beef? What's it for?'

She nodded towards the tank. 'Feeding them.'

'They eat meat now?'

'Right.'

'How d'you know?'

'Whaddya mean, how do I know? I'm a scientist, Rex. It's my business to find out these things.'

'You've fed them meat before, then? I ask because this is the first I've seen delivered.'

'Look, Rex, I've told you before. You can leave all that side of it to me.'

'Ah yes, but can I?' He pointed to the tank. 'Those things move fast, Wanda. They have sharp teeth. They eat meat. Suppose one escapes? It could kill somebody. And while we're on the subject of escapes.' He regarded her through narrowed eyes. 'I took a look at the door on that thing just now, and it isn't one door, it's two.'

The woman laughed. 'Of course it's two, you jerk. It's an airlock. The tank has a hydrogen atmosphere. If there was only one door the gas would escape the first time it was opened.'

Exley nodded. 'Right. I suppose I ought to have realized that, even as a non-scientist, but it never crossed my mind till I saw it a moment ago, and what's bothering me now is this. How was it possible for floaters to escape on at least half a dozen separate occasions when there were two doors and an airlock between them and freedom? I mean, anybody can forget to fasten a door – that's understandable, even if they forget more than once. But you'd have to have left both doors open, in which case you'd have lost all that nice hydrogen and your floaters would've died of oxygen poisoning.' He looked her in the eye. 'The only other way it could have happened is if somebody deliberately released a floater by herding the damn thing into the airlock and closing the inner door before opening the outer one.'

'Listen, Rex.' Free's voice was flat, her eyes chips of ice. 'What I've done here – everything I've done – has been necessary for my research and is no concern of yours. And don't think I don't know the way your mind's working, because I do. You're thinking about alien bacteria. Viruses. You're thinking these dragons are dangerous, and that now's the time to share our achievement with the world. Well – you can forget it. I'm not about to turn my work over to somebody who'll destroy it all, just when it's starting to get interesting.'

He'd backed down, of course, but after that Thursday morning you'd only have had to look at his face to know Rex Exley was a worried man.

T H I R T Y - N I N E

They were halfway up Tansy Road when the police car overtook them and pulled in. As they drew level, Constable Aspinall rolled down his window. 'Michelle?' They stopped and he said, 'Are you Michelle Fixby of sixteen Ragwort Drive?'

'Yes.'

He looked at the boy. 'You wouldn't by any chance be Benjamin Lockwood?'

Ben nodded. 'Yes, I would.'

'Lovely.' The policeman smiled. 'I've just come from your house. Your mother said you might be with Miss Fixby. I assume you know what this is about.'

Midge nodded. 'It's about Rudge, isn't it?'

Aspinall frowned. 'Rudge?'

'The Major's dog.'

'Oh yes, that's right. The spaniel. Didn't know his name. Hang on a tick.' He switched off the engine, unbelted himself and got out of the car. 'Couple of questions. You were in Pitney Wood when the dog was attacked, is that right?'

'Yes.'

'Did you witness the attack?'

'No, Rudge was out of sight but we heard it.'

'What did you hear exactly?'

'Well, Rudge sort of howled. Ben thought he'd got caught in a trap. Then he howled again and yelped a couple of times and then it went quiet.'

'You didn't hear anything else – another animal perhaps?'

'No.'

'So then what did you do?'

'We went towards the sound—'

'What sound?'

'Oh, there was this wet, snuffling sound. It made me think of something eating. A lion or something. And then we saw Rudge on the ground and this horrible thing on top of him, eating him.'

'Now, you say "this horrible thing". Can you describe it at all? For instance, how big was it?'

'Oh, it was—' She looked at Ben. 'This big?' She held her hand about half a metre above the pavement and Ben nodded. 'About that, yes. It was on top of Rudge and there were some bushes so it was hard to tell.'

'And what did it look like?'

'Well – it had a head like one of those fishes that lives very deep down in the ocean. You know – too big for its body, and a great big mouth full of sharp teeth, and little feet with claws and a long, tapering body like a dragon. That's what it reminded me of – a dragon.'

The policeman smiled. 'There are no dragons, son. Old Mr Tench thinks it was probably a big bird of some sort. Could it have been?'

'No!' Midge shook her head emphatically. 'No way. It didn't have feathers, it was smooth and sort of glistening, like it might be slimy.'

'What colour was it?'

'Oh, greyish, I think.'

'With some purple,' added Ben. 'You could see inside it a bit. It was—'

'Semi-transparent?' suggested the Constable.

'Yes, that's it.'

Aspinall smiled again. 'Look, you two. What you're describing sounds like something out of a TV horror movie. Now I'm not suggesting you're making anything up, but it's pretty dark in that wood. Are you absolutely sure that what you saw couldn't have been some enormous bird like a vulture, or a mammal such as a bear or wolf or puma, or even another dog?'

Midge shook her head again. Her mouth was a thin line. 'No, it was nothing like that, Mr Aspinall. It wasn't like anything you'd expect to see because it was an alien and I know where it came from.'

'An alien, eh? And where did it come from – Mars, I suppose?'

'No. Cansfield Farm.'

'Cansfield—?' The Constable laughed briefly, then frowned. 'Now look here, young woman. I'm prepared to believe that you saw something, in the dark under the trees, which looked to you, in your nervous state, like some sort of monster, but I'm not going to go to my Inspector in town and tell him Dan Cansfield's lost an alien and it's loose in Pitney Wood.' He pocketed his notebook, opened the car door and looked at the pair. 'If there's nothing else you can tell me, I'll get off. Thanks for your help.'

'Oh, but—' Midge started towards him but he swung himself into the driver's seat, slammed the door and started the engine.

They watched as the car rolled forward, gathering speed. Then they looked at each other, Midge pulled a face and they moved on towards Ragwort Drive.

They hadn't been in the house two minutes when the phone rang. Midge nodded towards the fridge. 'Get a couple of Cokes out, Ben, while I get that.' She went out into the hallway but returned almost at once. 'It's for you, Ben. Your dad.'

Ben sighed. 'It figures.' He put on a silly voice. 'The police have been looking for you, Ben. What have you been doing?' Midge laughed, opening cans.

'Hello, Dad.'

'Ben. Constable Aspinall was here asking for you.'

'I know. We've seen him.'

155

'What did he want with you, Ben. You haven't been up to anything, have you?'

'Yes, Dad. Me and Midge robbed a bank, so it's not Bonnie and Clyde any more, it's Midgie and Ben.'

'Don't be cheeky, Ben. Your mother's worried sick.'

Briefly, Ben outlined the morning's events without mentioning the word 'dragon'. When he'd finished, his father said, 'Well, listen, son. Stay away from the wood for the time being, and don't go over the fields. There's obviously a dangerous animal about and I don't want you running into it again. Lunch is almost ready, by the way, if you're coming home.'

'I don't fancy lunch, Dad. Not after – you know?'

'Oh, right. I can understand that. I'll see you later on then. And remember what I said. Keep to the village.'

Ben went back to the kitchen and sat at the table. Midge slid a Coke across. 'What did your dad want?'

'What d'you think? I told him we robbed a bank. He wasn't amused.'

She smiled. 'My dad would've said, "Well, you'll just have to sort it out for yourself, love. Your mother and I are busy." '

'He wouldn't.'

'He would.'

They sipped Coke and talked. Somebody knocked on the front door. Midge frowned. 'Who the heck's this?' She went to see and returned with a red-headed girl of seventeen or eighteen. 'Ben, this is Sharon Deeping. She's a reporter.'

The girl smiled. 'I'm not a real reporter, Ben. I'm still at school. I cover Little Pitney for the *Journal*, that's all.'

Ben looked at her. 'Are you related to Ginger Deeping at our school?'

'Yes, he's my brother.' The girl smiled. 'Mind if I sit down?'

'Oh, sorry, yes.' Midge pulled out a chair. 'Would you like a Coke?'

'No thanks. I've come about the dog that was killed. You saw it, didn't you?'

Midge and Ben eyed each other. They knew the full story could get them into big trouble, but surely this was their one chance to get someone interested in the truth.

They told their story. They explained Midge's tadpole theory. They told Sharon of their nocturnal visits to Cansfield Farm and about what they'd seen there. Sharon scribbled shorthand notes on a pad. 'Hmm,' she said, when she had it all down. 'Thanks, you two. Interesting angle, the dragon bit.'

'What d'you mean, angle?' Midge asked.

'Well, stories about animals being savaged by other animals are ten a penny, especially where there are sheep, but the culprit's nearly always a dog. Very occasionally it'll be something that's escaped from somewhere – a wolf or a puma. But a dragon!' She grinned. 'Well – that's what's known as an angle, Midge. Something which makes an ordinary story that bit different.'

'It's all true, you know.'

'Oh, I'm not doubting it, love.'

'So you'll print it then – about Cansfield Farm and all?'

Sharon laughed. 'Well, I've got it all down, but I doubt whether they'll print it. There's no proof, you see. No confirmation. Dan Cansfield could sue the *Journal* for thousands and he'd do it, too.'

'But we were there,' protested Ben. 'We saw those things. And anyway, what would Free and Exley be doing at Cansfield Farm if there wasn't something funny going on?'

The reporter smiled. 'I'll pass it on,' she promised. 'But it'll be up to the editor whether it gets in the paper, and I wouldn't be too hopeful if I were you.'

When Sharon Deeping had gone, Ben said, 'What now, Midge? If no-one will believe us, somebody's going to get killed.'

Midge looked at him. 'You heard Sharon, Ben. Proof. Confirmation. One more midnight expedition, this time with a camera. And the sooner we do it, the better.'

FORTY

Ben didn't fancy Cansfield again, but there was one consolation. This time they'd be able to choose a night when Barry was on guard. Monday was out anyway, because it was the Fixbys' night off and Midge wasn't sure she'd get out of the house, and when Ben spoke to Barry at the Village Hall on Monday lunchtime it turned out his next stint was Wednesday. 'I'm pig-sick of it,' he grumbled. 'When are you and that girlfriend of yours gonna get the fuzz in, Locky?'

Ben told him they were working on it and went up to Tarkington's to phone Midge. 'It's on for Wednesday,' he said. 'But Barry says things have changed. We've got to meet him at the playing field tomorrow morning and he'll tell us all about it.' As he left the box, Frieda Cansfield came staggering out of the mini-market with four bulging carriers. 'Hello, Mrs Cansfield,' Ben said brightly. 'Let me take a couple of those for you.'

'Oh, don't trouble yourself, dear. I can manage.'

'It's no trouble – I'm practising to be a gentleman.'

The carriers weighed a ton. As they tottered towards the old Suzuki, Ben said, 'What on earth have you been buying, Mrs Cansfield – lead shot?'

The woman's smile was strained. 'It's mostly meat, dear. We've got – visitors.'

Yes I know, thought Ben. From outer space. You'll have two more on Wednesday night and, soon after that, all being well, you'll get a sudden visit from a whole bunch of people in blue uniforms.

He didn't say any of this. What he said was, 'I hope your visitors appreciate all the trouble and expense, Mrs Cansfield.' He wondered if that was cheeky, and decided it probably was.

He helped her stow the carriers in the back of the Suzuki and watched as the vehicle rattled off, belching smoke.

The *Journal* would be delivered to the house at tea-time, but Ben couldn't wait. He went into Tarkington's and picked up a copy. Phyllis Tarkington smirked as she gave him the change. 'What's it like to be famous, Ben?'

Her question caught him off-balance and he mumbled, 'Great, thanks,' or something equally prattish and hurried outside, cheeks burning.

It hadn't made the headlines but it was on the front page – a paragraph near the bottom, headed 'Dog Death – Dragon?' He skimmed it, and swore under his breath. There was nothing about Cansfield or corn circles. Rudge's death was done straight, but Sharon Deeping had given the dragon bit a tongue-in-cheek treatment which made Midge and himself look silly, he thought. 'Sharon Deeping,' he muttered, taking the paper into the phone-box, 'you're worse than your spasmo brother.'

He called Midge, read the item to her and said, 'We'd have been better not talking to her at all.'

'Oh, I dunno,' said Midge. 'I know she's done it nudge-nudge, Ben, but at least there's a suggestion that what killed Rudge might have been something unusual, and you never know who might read it.'

Ben left the phone-box with his copy of the *Journal* under his arm. He was about to cross High Street when a red Sierra pulled in near him. The driver stuck his head out of the window and called to him in an American accent. 'Pardon me, son.'

Ben went over. Tourist, he thought, looking for Stonehenge or Avebury or somewhere. He put on his friendly smile. 'Can I help you?'

'I hope so. I'm looking for a place called Cansfield Farm. Do you know it?'

Ben swallowed. 'Yes. Yes, I do.' He pointed. 'When you get through the village, keep looking to your right. It's the first farm. There's no sign, but you'll

161

see a break in the hedge and a track with a tractor blocking it. That's Cansfield Farm.'

The man nodded. 'I'm obliged to you, son. Take care now.'

Ben watched the Sierra till it passed from view, then crossed over and walked home, wondering why the American would be visiting Cansfield. With his grey suit and smart blue tie, he didn't look much like a tourist.

FORTY-ONE

Rex Exley made it his business to read through his hosts' copy of the *Journal* every tea-time, not because he particularly admired the paper, but to check that nothing was happening in Little Pitney which he ought to know about. He looked particularly for corn circle stories and items about the arrival of strangers, and was greatly relieved if he found none.

It was Dan's unsociable habit to read the paper while eating and to pass it across the table to Exley when he'd finished. Sometimes, Rex would read bits aloud to Wanda, but he wouldn't be doing that any more because Wanda now insisted on having all her meals brought to her in the barn. So, when he spotted Sharon Deeping's item that Monday, he couldn't immediately share it with her. He drank his tea more quickly than usual, refused a second cup and left the table.

Wanda had finished tea and was dabbing her lips with a Kleenex when Rex strode into the cubicle, waving the paper. 'Have you seen this?' he demanded. The woman balled up the Kleenex, lobbed it into a wastepaper basket and said, 'Not if it's today's, Rex. Why?'

'Why?' He thrust it at her, jabbing at the item with a finger. 'Look at that.'

Wanda read the piece while he bent over her. When she'd finished, she gave him a quizzical look. 'Yeah – so what?'

'So what's this dragon the kids say they saw?'

'How should I know? You know how kids are – overactive imaginations.'

'Come off it, Wanda. Look at that description. Are you going to tell me they didn't see one of those monsters you've got in there?'

She shook her head. 'I'm not going to tell you that, Rex.'

He threw the paper on the floor. 'Good grief, woman, are you completely mad? Those things are carnivorous. They kill. And you released one, didn't you? You let one out.'

'So?'

'Why, Wanda? Didn't you realize it was bound to be seen? Do you want the police combing the countryside, maybe calling here? It's not exactly what we need right now, is it?'

Wanda half turned her swivel chair and stood up. 'Now you listen to me, Rex. I'm not crazy. There's a good reason for everything I do. Those animals need intense cold and a hydrogen atmosphere. Release one, and two things happen. First, it dies of oxygen poisoning within a short time, and second, its tissues dissolve and seep away into the soil. In a few hours, no trace of it remains.'

'So why release it in the first place?'

'In order to know, Rex.'

'Know what, for crying out loud?'

'All kinds of things. How it copes with low gravity and a hostile environment. How it travels. Finds its food. How long it takes the oxygen to kill it. Stuff like that.'

'And for that you're prepared to put the lives of innocent people at risk?'

'You bet I am. I'm gonna know all there is to know about these beauties before some creep from NASA comes along and creams 'em, and for that there's nothing I won't do.'

Exley shook his head. 'You are mad, Wanda. This started out as a legitimate project – undoubtedly the most original and exciting project in the annals of biology. All right, so you stole the eggs or spawn or whatever from NASA because they ordered it destroyed. That was unethical and probably illegal but you had your reasons and I sympathized. The advancement of human knowledge, you said, combined with the enrichment and exaltation of Wanda

Free. And why not? So I put up the money. Found you a quiet place. Took care of everything so you could concentrate on your work. And you succeeded, Wanda. Working in an old barn with the simplest equipment, you hatched out the first extraterrestrial life-form this planet has ever seen and raised it to maturity. All that was left to do was show the world, and fame and fortune would follow as night follows day. But have you done it? No. And why? Because you've flipped your lid, Wanda, that's why. Lost your marbles.'

The woman gazed at him. 'They dumped me, Rex. The Jupiter series was my baby. The spawn was mine and they said, "Destroy it. We'll get more, deliver it to Orbiter so the guys out there can work on it." And when I asked to be assigned to Orbiter they said, "Request denied."' She laughed wildly. 'Request denied. Well, I'll show 'em, Rex. A few more days, that's all I need.' She smiled. 'Come see 'em, Rex.' She moved towards the tank, her tone wheedling. 'Come look at my beautiful babies.' But when she turned round, Rex Exley had gone.

Rex was now deeply worried. The thing he'd dreaded all along was beginning to happen. It wasn't just nosy kids any more, or reporters sniffing out the curious and the novel with which to entertain their brain-dead readers. The authorities were becoming involved. The police.

And Wanda's mad, he told himself, as he left the

barn and walked aimlessly down the pathway between the outbuildings and the house. Perhaps she's
been mad all along, but now it's obvious. Scientists
have to be cold, dispassionate operators to some ex-
tent, I know that. They can't afford to let sentiment
interfere with their work, but they accept certain re-
sponsibilities. They don't conduct experiments which
they know will endanger the public, even where such
experiments might save years of work. Wanda does.
She knew there was a chance those floaters might be
carrying some alien virus but she released them, just
to see what would happen. She knows her monsters
move fast, have sharp teeth and eat flesh, but she wired
one up and let it out to satisfy her curiosity.

Exley's reverie was broken when the side door of
the house opened and Dan Cansfield emerged.

'Excuse me, Mr Exley. Can I have a word?'

'Yes, of course.'

'It's about the livestock.'

Exley looked at him sharply. 'Not more money,
Mr Cansfield?'

The farmer shook his head. 'No, sir. Money don't
matter no more. I want you out.'

'I beg your pardon?'

'You heard me, Mr Exley. I seen the bit in the paper,
and I wondered. Then I seen you take the paper up
the barn so I sent the boy to listen, and from what he
could make out them animals ain't the same. Killers
was the word, he says, and your friend's letting 'em
loose to worry stock and kill folks for all she cares.

It's in the paper and the police're interested and that's where I get off.'

'You can't.' Exley shook his head. 'We have an agreement. You've been involved from the start and you've no choice now but to see it through.'

Fear showed in the farmer's eyes. 'Killing's not in the agreement, Mr Exley, nor dragons from Jupiter neither. That woman's off her head and I want the pair of you off my place Thursday morning at the latest or I go to the coppers myself.'

Exley watched dumbly as Cansfield went in and slammed the door. Everything's falling apart, he told himself. I must keep a grip on myself. Think. He felt that his skull might burst. He shook his head and moved on down the path. He leaned on a gatepost with his hands in his pockets, gazing absently at the traffic and trying to get his head together.

Think. A few more days, Wanda says. Mind you she's said that before, but still. When I tell her about Cansfield it's bound to gee her up a bit. Or is it? She's barmy, remember. She might decide to shoot the blighter, take over the farm.

No. I reckon if she'll give me a definite date for finishing, I'll be able to stall old Dan. Money's the key. He says it doesn't matter any more but I don't believe him. He's crazy about the stuff. What shall we say – a hundred a day for every day after Thursday? Yes, I fancy he'll go for that.

And then there's the fuzz on the track of the mystery beast, but not too seriously. They've only the kids' description and they know what kids are like. They'll be looking for a dog.

So. Calm down, Rex old lad. Calm Wanda down. Tranquillize Dan with banknotes. Think of the cash you've put into this thing and hang on. Don't panic.

He'd managed to make himself feel pretty good when the red Sierra pulled into the kerb and the driver stuck his head out. 'Pardon me, sir?'

'Yes?' Yankee tourist, Rex. Nothing to worry about.

'Is this Cansfield Farm?'

'Yes.' Steady, old chap. 'Yes, it is. Why?' Shouldn't have asked that. Sounds aggressive.

The American smiled. 'I read some stuff in the papers. Corn circles. This is where it happened, right?'

Exley nodded. 'Hoax. Young Farmers. Gone now. Nothing to see.' Buzz off, he thought. Go photograph some morris dancers.

The man looked crestfallen for a moment, then smiled and said, 'Oh well, doesn't matter.' He was unfastening his seat-belt. Just push off, thought Exley. Don't get out of the car. But then the American was out. He waved a hand to indicate the farm. 'This your place?'

Exley shook his head. 'I just work here.'

'Ah, right.' He grinned. 'I'm Ed Lester, by the way.'

'Smith,' grunted Exley. 'Er – Jim.'

'Hi, Jim.' The Yank thrust out a paw. They shook. The man looked Exley in the eye. 'What d'you think causes 'em?'

'I told you. Young Farmers.'

'Really? No little green men?'

'No.'

'Ah-ha. And there's nothing to see now, huh?'

'Nothing at all.'

'Hmm. Might as well move on then, I guess.' Exley felt a surge of relief. There was something about Ed Lester that made him feel uneasy. The way his eyes moved about all the time as though he might be searching for something, even while he was speaking. He seemed to be talking about one thing and thinking about another. And his clothes were wrong. Who wore a suit and tie to drive around on holiday? He forced a smile. 'I'm afraid you might as well, Mr Lester. Sorry I couldn't be more help.'

'Oh, that's all right.' The man smiled. 'Nice meeting you, Mr Jones.'

Even as they shook hands, he was looking past Exley towards the farm.

It wasn't till the Sierra had roared off towards Warminster that Exley realized the American had called him Jones and he hadn't corrected him.

FORTY-TWO

Wanda closed the barn door and secured it. Then she picked up one of the plastic carriers, took it across to the tank and unfastened the outer door. She stepped inside, set the carrier down and pulled the door closed. Its locking mechanism activated a switch which flooded the airlock with blue light. As this light came on, the creatures inside the tank flung themselves at the inner door and the woman heard a series of impacts followed by scrabbling, scratching noises as they attacked its frost-furred surface with fang and claw. She smiled. 'It's all right,' she crooned. 'I'm here with your supper, my beautiful darlings.'

She lifted down her breathing apparatus from the hook on the wall. The twin cylinders were cumbersome, the paraphernalia of straps, clips and face mask difficult to manage in the cramped space. She shrugged herself with difficulty into the web harness, clipped on the mask and turned to the inner door.

As they felt it move, the frenzied aliens thrust their slavering mouths at the slowly widening slot between the door and its housing. The airlock walls reverberated to their screeching din as each creature struggled to squeeze itself through. When the opening was twenty centimetres wide, an automatic restraint came into operation, preventing the door from opening further. Laughing into her mask, Wanda Free began scooping meat from the carrier and flinging it through the gap. Some pieces went directly into the jaws of her pets but most of it flew past to land on the floor. One by one, the creatures left off attacking the door in order to pounce on these rags and gobbets of flesh. Soon the bag was empty and the ravenous beasts were fighting one another over scraps on the blood-smeared floor. The woman jabbed a button with a gory finger and the door closed with a clunk, cutting off the noise of their feeding.

In the blue silence she stripped off the clumsy apparatus and hung it up. As the outer door opened, the light went off and Free left the airlock, taking the crumpled, sticky-wet carrier with her. She closed the door, checked it and stayed to watch her pets through a port. She murmured softly to herself as she watched, and once or twice she laughed out loud. When the last morsel of food had gone and the fun was over, she left the port and crossed to the cubicle, dropping the carrier into a wastepaper bin. 'Such naughty crea-tures,' she sighed. 'So violent, but then who can blame them? Dead meat nourishes but there's no stimulus in it – no challenge.' She chuckled. 'Live prey's the thing, and I've a hunch there'll be some available in the near future.'

The barn echoed to her laughter as she rinsed her hands in a bucket of cold water and began to pre-pare for bed.

FORTY-THREE

Ben left the house at half-past eight Tuesday morning and crossed the road. There was a bit of haze, but the sun was breaking through and it would be hot later on. Midge was looking at a display of beachwear, dark glasses and suntan lotion in Tarkington's window. She saw his reflection and turned.

'Hi, Ben.'

'Hi yourself. You going away or what?'

'No. We've been away, remember? I was just fancying these sunglasses – the ones with the green frames.'

'Ugh! All your taste's in your mouth, girl.'

'Don't be cheeky.'

They walked on towards the school. Ben had arranged to see Barry on the playing field, but when they got there he hadn't arrived. The grass was still dewy so they strolled round the perimeter, chatting. It was ten past nine and the sun had burned off most of the haze when Barry arrived. Wayne Daykin and Ginger Deeping were with him, but when he spotted Midge and Ben and came across, they stayed behind.

'Hi, Barry.'

The boy nodded. 'You still on for tomorrow, Midge?'

She pulled a face. 'Depends what's changed, Barry. Ben says you've something to tell us.'

Barry nodded. 'I have. I hope it won't put you off though.'

'What is it?' The dew had evaporated. Midge plonked herself down and the two boys joined her.

'It's that woman.' Barry looked down, plucking nervously at some blades of grass. 'She's gone off her nut. Don't trust nobody. Sleeps in the barn, has her grub there, everything.' He paused, shredding grass. 'Them floaters've changed. I've not seen 'em – she won't let anybody near – but they eat meat now. Loads of it. She makes Mum fetch it from Tarkington's. Everybody looks at her funny when she goes in.'

'We've seen a floater,' said Ben. He was absolutely sure now. 'It was horrible. Like a dragon.'

Barry nodded. 'She lets 'em out. I heard her talking to Exley. That's how I know she's off her nut. Listen.' He threw down the tuft of grass he'd been playing with and wrapped his arms round his knees. 'I think I know how to get her out of the barn, but it wouldn't be for long and it's dangerous. She's a bag of nerves and she's got a gun. How long would you need?'

Midge shrugged. 'A minute or two. Time to get a shot of the tank and a couple through the window.'

Barry looked at her. 'It'll be dark, y'know.'

'That's OK. Camera's got flash. How are you going to get her out?'

'Voices, and the gun.'

'Gun?'

'Yes. Look. We're near the barn, right? I shout, like I've spotted intruders. You shout to Ben, a warning, and he shouts back. By this time she'll be up and panicking. I fire a shot. She comes out to see what's happening. I let 'er see me go into one of the outbuildings like I've shot somebody in there or got 'em cornered. She runs across to see and you slip into the barn. I reckon I could have her searching the building for a minute or so, and Dad'll probably be there by then too.'

Midge gazed at him. 'And what about after? Won't you get in terrible trouble?'

'Why? I saw intruders, chased 'em, they gave me the slip in the dark. Only way I'll be in trouble is if they catch you in the barn.'

'Ooh, don't!' Midge shivered. 'I think we should leave something behind so they know we were there. Not in the barn, of course. Outside. How about my torch? I could've dropped it when you shot at me.'

Barry grinned. 'I like it.'

'Right,' said Midge. 'So we'll see you beside the tractor in the driveway at two o'clock Thursday morning. If anything changes in the meantime, give me a ring at home. OK?'

'OK.'

They stood up. Barry went off to find Wayne and Ginger, who had got fed up and gone off somewhere. Ben and Midge left the field and strolled back along High Street. It was hot. They paused at Tarkington's for Midge to have another look at the sunglasses. 'Tell you what,' said Ben. 'Thursday morning, if everything's gone right, I'll buy 'em for you.'

'I'll let you.' The Mona Lisa smile was strained. 'If.'

F O R T Y - F O U R

Tuesday evening, early. Rex Exley, at the barn door, was trying to talk to his partner.

'Wanda?'

'Go away, Rex.'

'I've got to talk to you. It's desperately important.'

'I'm in bed.'

'But it's only ten to eight.'

'What're you – the talking clock? I'm tired.'

'D'you think I'm not? I was on guard last night.'

'So go to bed, Rex.'

'Dan's kicking us out, Wanda. He wants us gone by Thursday.'

'On the money we're paying him? Tell him to go take a running jump.'

'He'll go to the police.'

'No, he won't. He's in this up to the eyeballs and he knows it.'

'He'll use force, then.'

'Let him try. I'm armed. Ask him how he proposes to get me out of this barn.'

'Wanda, you can't—'

'Oh, but I can. You just watch me.'

'Yes, but—'

'Good night, Rex.'

FORTY - FIVE

Wednesday morning at Ben's place. The Lockwoods at breakfast. Ben had hardly slept and here it was, the big day. He thought, will I be sitting here tomorrow morning, or will I be— He shivered, wondering whether it might be worth telling Mum and Dad about Cansfield. If I can make them believe me, he thought, maybe they'll talk to Ken Aspinall and we won't have to go tonight.

'Mum?'

'Yes, dear?'

'We weren't mistaken, Midge and me. It was a monster we saw, and it did come from Cansfield.'

'Ben.'

'Yes, Dad?'

'We've been over all this. It was dark under the

180

trees, and seeing poor old Rudge like that was a terrible shock. It's not surprising the creature looked like a monster to you. As for the rest of your tale – well, I put it down to your spending your time with the Fixby girl. She's an odd child, and she's obviously got you involved in a fantasy she's playing out.'

'No, Dad, it's not a fantasy. What about Rex Exley and Wanda Free? If it's a fantasy, how come they're real?'

'Listen, son. You saw Frieda Cansfield with lots of shopping and she told you they've got visitors. You told me that yourself.'

'I know, but—'

'Now, that's enough, Ben. Your mother and I realize that the awful business with Rudge has upset you, but you must believe me when I tell you it will fade. In a few days' time you'll be running around, enjoying the holidays as though none of it ever happened.'

'I hope you're right, Dad.'

Wednesday morning at Midge's. The Fixbys at breakfast. Midge had eaten nothing, but nobody noticed. She was pale, and there were dark rings under her eyes and nobody noticed this either.

Midge thought, I don't want to go to Cansfield tonight. It's not my job. The police should go there, look around. That's all it would take.

'Mum?'

'Yes, dear?'

'It's true you know, about the monster. We did see it, and there are others at Cansfield Farm.'

'Yes, Midge, I'm sure there are. If you've finished breakfast I'd like you to take these to the post for me. They'll catch the first collection if you run.'

'Oh, Mum, won't you listen, just for once?'

'Midge!'

'Yes, Dad?'

'Stop being rude to your mother and take the letters. We're running a business here, there's no time for your nonsense.'

'I suppose I'll just have to risk my life, then.'

'I'll risk your life, young woman, if you're not through that door in five seconds flat.'

'Yes, Dad.'

I'm surprised you even remember my name, Dad.

F O R T Y - S I X

It was weird, that Wednesday. Dreamlike. They met at ten in the morning by arrangement, outside Tarkington's. The window display had been changed. The green sunglasses were gone, along with the rest of the holiday stuff. Uniform skirts and blouses now filled the space, and striped ties and satchels and sensible shoes. On an easel was a miniature blackboard with 'Back to School' chalked on it. It seemed like an omen.

'I tried—' Ben began.

'To tell your parents?' interrupted Midge. 'I know. So did I.'

It was going to be hot again. They walked, without destination, hardly speaking. The playing field. The churchyard. The shelter. The car park of the

Goose. It felt to Ben like saying goodbye.

When they'd been everywhere they sat in the shelter and finalized arrangements. One-thirty in the morning. Here. Midge to bring her camera (she'd bought a film that morning at Tarkington's) and her torch to throw down for Barry. Ben needn't bring anything except himself. They'd split up now, spend the afternoon at home (saying goodbye? wondered Ben) and get an early night.

They got up and went out into the dusty glare, the stream of holiday traffic. At the end of Tansy Road they squeezed hands.

'The glasses'll still be there,' said Ben. 'Inside the shop.'

Midge smiled and nodded.

'Barry?' Moonlight cast the tractor's shadow black on silver grass.

'Here.' The boy separated himself from the machine. 'You're late. I thought you weren't coming.' Their whispering seemed loud in the airless night.

'Sorry,' murmured Ben. 'My fault. Dad fancied a midnight swig.'

'Don't matter. Everything's quiet. She locked herself in at eight.'

They moved up the track, their shadows beside them. Somewhere a barn owl called. Ben jumped, Barry pointed his shotgun towards the sound, and Midge giggled. Further up, the shadow of the house lay across the path and they went slowly, Barry in the lead. Bracken, the dog, accustomed now to footfalls in the night, sounded no alarm.

The barn loomed. Barry stopped, holding up a hand for them to do the same. They looked at him.

'Right.' His voice was scarcely audible. 'The barn door's got a little door in it. She'll come out of that, and with any luck she'll leave it open. If she don't – if she stays to lock it – the operation's off. If that happens, you run and don't look back. Got it?'

Midge nodded.

'Good. If she leaves it open, you nip in quick, do what you have to do and get out. Don't hang about, 'cause if you're caught and split on me I'll deny everything and you'll die. OK?'

'OK,' breathed Ben.

'Right. Wait here. I'll go over by the goose-house and shout. As soon as you hear me, you call out to each other and I fire this thing. That should bring her out. I'll make like I've got somebody cornered in the goose-house, and she'll come running with her gun. I'll make sure there's plenty of racket so when Dad and Exley leave the house, they'll know where to come.' He looked at Midge. 'Got that torch?' She handed it to him and he forced a grin. 'See you tomorrow.'

They followed him with their eyes till he merged with the shadow of the goose-house. Ben reached for Midge's hand and squeezed it briefly. Fantasy, his father had said. If only it were.

'Hey, you!' The pair jumped as Barry's voice split the night. 'What you doing there? Stop or I'll fire.'

'Jim!' screamed Midge. 'Look out, Jim, he's got a gun.'

Jim? Ben hesitated for an instant, then the penny dropped. 'Run, Maggie!' he cried. 'That way. I'm right behind you.'

Barry yelled again. 'Hold it right there, you interferin' creepazoid, or I'll blow your head off.'

He was still shouting when the little door flew open and Free stumbled out, wearing striped pyjamas and brandishing an automatic. 'What is it?' she screeched. 'Where the heck are you, kid?'

'Over here, Miss Free,' cried Barry. 'Quick.' The woman ran towards the goose-house, leaving the door wide open.

'Come on, Ben,' hissed Midge. 'This is it.'

F O R T Y - S E V E N

Len Tench liked a nice bit of rabbit, and there were hundreds of rabbits in Pitney Wood. Technically they belonged to Major Fairbairn, but one man couldn't possibly use hundreds of rabbits, and besides the Major was more of a pheasant man. So Len was often to be found late at night in the wood, inspecting his snares and resetting them.

It was while he was doing this, very late that Wednesday night, that he came upon Ben and Midge's monster. It was dead, but it was definitely a monster, and Len spent some time examining it by the light from his torch.

He didn't know what to do. The police ought to be informed, and the Major would be interested, but how was he to explain his presence at midnight in Pitney

Wood? Couldn't sleep. Too hot. Decided to go for a walk. Well, provided he took his bag home first, they couldn't prove different, could they?

And that's exactly what he did. The Major was none too pleased when his gardener woke the household at half-past one in the morning, but when Len told him he'd found Rudge's killer, and described it, he pulled on some clothes and followed the man into the wood.

It was just after two when the Major phoned Ken Aspinall at home. The Constable was out, but his wife told the Major she'd give him the message the minute he came in, though she thought he'd probably wait till morning to visit the scene. After all, the monster wasn't likely to go anywhere, was it?

Wendy Aspinall had just put the phone down when it rang again. Matthew Lockwood sounded frightened. He told her he'd got out of bed to go to the bathroom, checked his son's room and found the kid wasn't there. He'd searched the house then woken his wife, who was frantic.

In emergencies, Wendy was able to contact her husband by radio. Emergencies were few and far between in Little Pitney, but this was one. She called him. He was to go to number eight, High Street. Young Ben Lockwood was missing. Oh, and the Major had called. Something about a dead monster.

As he drove along High Street, a little bell rang in the Constable's brain. He'd questioned young Lockwood last Sunday about the Major's dog. Now what was it the kid had said? 'It wasn't like anything you'd expect to see because it was an alien and I know where it came from.' *I know where it came from.* As he opened the freshly painted gate of number eight, Ken Aspinall was smiling.

FORTY-EIGHT

It wasn't completely dark inside the barn. Something in the cubicle shed a weak yellow light, and a faint bluish radiance marked the positions of viewing ports in the walls of the tank.

'Stay here,' said Midge, fiddling briefly with her camera. 'Watch the door.' Ben nodded as the girl raised the instrument and squinted through the viewfinder. 'Look away,' she warned. The flash seemed terrifically bright. Ben looked out. Voices reached him from the direction of the goose-house and there was a scraping, clattering noise like something heavy being shifted. Inside the house, invisible from the barn, Bracken was barking steadily.

Midge was at the tank, her head, hands and shoulders silhouetted against a port as she aimed her camera at something inside. Ben turned away, managing to pull the barn door to just before the flash. He peered through the crack. The goose-house door was open and somebody was using a torch inside. A shout, some barking and the rhythmic thud of a heavy runner told him that somebody was approaching from the house. Bracken appeared, streaking towards the goose-house, followed a moment later by Dan.

Ben watched. As Dan approached the goose-house, Wanda Free appeared in its doorway, dragging Barry by the collar of his shirt. At the same moment Rex Exley appeared, shrugging himself into a jacket as he ran.

'Midge!' As Ben turned to hiss a warning, the flash went off again, half blinding him. 'She's got Barry!' he cried. 'I think she's coming this way.' A globe of vivid green light floated before Ben's eyes, impairing his vision so that he could hardly find the door. He heard Free call to someone, 'Here – take this – watch him!' He groped for the door and was halfway through when his foot caught the raised threshold and he fell. Midge, following at speed, tripped over him and performed a sort of running dive, her balance gone. As she toppled forward she threw out her arms which, encountering something more solid than air, wrapped themselves round it. Midge heard a wild laugh and opened her eyes to find herself hugging Wanda's knees while the muzzle of the woman's automatic ground into her left ear.

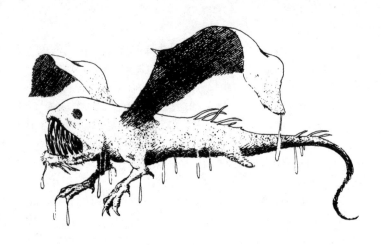

FORTY-NINE

Emma Lockwood wasn't smiling. Slumped on the settee in towelling robe and slippers, with her hair down and the marks of weeping on her face, she looked ravaged. In his line of work, Ken Aspinall saw a lot of people in her condition but he'd never really got used to it. He was a young man, and there was something embarrassing about playing comforter to a distraught person older than oneself.

Matthew Lockwood looked at him. 'So you think he might have gone to Dan Cansfield's place?'

Aspinall nodded. 'Seems likely, yes. He mentioned the farm to both of us in connection with this monster story, didn't he?'

'Yes. So hadn't we better get out there? Dan

Cansfield doesn't take kindly to trespassers in daylight. God knows what he might do at three in the morning.'

The policeman nodded. 'I'll drive out and take a look around, but first I want to check on the girl, Michelle Fixby. She was with your lad when I spoke to him, and from what you say she's mixed up in this monster thing too. I wonder if she's tucked up in her bed right now.'

Ben's mother looked at her husband. 'Call the Fixbys, Matt. Ask them.'

'Good idea, Emma.' He glanced at the policeman. 'That all right with you?'

Aspinall nodded. 'Certainly. I hope they hear it ringing, that's all.'

Ben's father left the room. Aspinall looked at the distressed woman. 'Ben's a bright lad, Mrs Lockwood,' he said. 'He'll be all right.' He wished he felt as confident as he sounded. The more he thought about this monster business, the less far-fetched it was beginning to seem, especially since the Major had mentioned the word 'monster' to Wendy. Major Fairbairn wasn't the hysterical sort. He didn't go round imagining things. If he described something he'd seen as a monster, it was a fair bet he'd seen something pretty unusual.

The policeman's train of thought was broken by Lockwood's return. 'She's not there,' he said. Fixby seems to think she must have taken his camera with her.'

'Right, well I'm going to call up some assistance from the Warminster Force and we'll get out to Cansfield straightaway. You wait here in case he returns, and don't worry. There's two of them and they're sensible kids. They'll be all right.'

F I F T Y

'On your feet, girl, now!' The woman seized a fistful of Midge's collar and half-hauled her erect. Ben rose to his knees and found himself looking up the muzzle of the exabiologist's gun. 'You. Pick that up.' Free moved the gun so that it pointed to Midge's fallen camera. Ben retrieved the instrument and stood up. 'Put it by my foot.' He did so and she stamped on it, twice. She was wearing flimsy-looking slippers but the camera burst open, exposing the film.

Keeping the gun pointed at Ben and without loosing her hold on Midge's collar, the woman turned her head. 'Barry Cansfield, get over here fast!' Ben looked past her. Over by the goose-house, Rex Exley had Barry and Dan covered with the farmer's shotgun. Barry looked at Exley, who made a small sideways

195

motion with the gun to show him he could go. Ben hoped Barry would run for it, fetch help, but with bright moonlight plus Rex's gun behind him, and Wanda's in front of him, there was no chance.

When Barry drew near, Wanda let Midge go and motioned the two of them to join Ben.

'Now.' She smiled at the three of them like a teacher at the start of a lesson. 'I have three little nuisances to dispose of and a tankful of ravenous carnivores to feed. What do you suppose a resourceful person might do in a situation like that? Barry?' She cocked her head on one side as though expecting his answer.

She's crazy, thought Midge. Terror washed over her so that she almost fell down. She knew the answer all right, and she could tell by Ben's face that he did too. Barry wasn't sure, but the way he was chewing his lip and glancing towards the barn showed he was working it out. Midge was getting her head together to run for it when Exley called out, 'Wanda!' He took a couple of steps towards her. 'You can't—'

'OH YES I CAN!' He recoiled from the blast of her scream. She smiled at the sight of his shocked face and purred, 'You know, Rex, you're gonna have to stop telling me what I can and cannot do, or you might just find yourself inside that tank with the rest of the nuisances.' She turned back to the children. 'OK, kids, this is it – the moment you've been waiting for. You've shown an awful lot of interest in my pets over the past weeks. Now you're going to meet 'em. Start walking.'

'Hey!' Dan Cansfield frowned at Exley. 'What

was that about? Where's she taking them kids?'

Exley looked towards the barn. The children were already inside. As he watched, Free stepped over the threshold and out of sight. He gulped. 'I think – I'm afraid she means to feed them to her pets.' He still had the farmer covered but his heart wasn't in it.

'You what?' Cansfield roared, eyeing the gun. 'Well do something, man, for Pete's sake – she's your partner.'

Exley shrugged. 'I'm not tackling her, Cansfield. She's completely barmy and I've seen her shoot.' He lowered the gun. 'You can go if you like.'

Cansfield hesitated for a moment then ran, not to the barn but towards the house. Exley gazed towards the barn, shook his head and followed the farmer.

'Frieda!' Frieda Cansfield came scurrying as her husband burst, bellowing, through the kitchen door. 'Get on the blower – police. Free's got Barry and some other kids in the barn.'

His wife's eyes darted round the room. 'Barry? She's not took my Barry?'

'Yes, he's one of 'em.'

'And you let her?'

'She's got a gun, you daft beggar. What's I supposed to do – get myself shot? Get on that phone, woman, 'fore it's too late.'

'Damn the phone!' The farmer's jaw sagged as his wife screamed at him. Frieda never talked back. Not to him. He winced as she shouted, 'No time for that, you great soft article. Get outa my way!' She pushed past him, grabbed her anorak in the porch and ran outside, almost colliding with Exley. The old Suzuki stood in an outbuilding. She ran to it, wrenched open its door and clambered into the driver's seat.

Exley, misreading the woman's intentions, sprinted to the vehicle as its engine roared into life. 'I don't know where you're going,' he gasped, diving into the passenger seat, 'but you can drop me off in Warminster.'

Frieda made no reply. She put the vehicle into gear, rolled it clear of the outhouse, turned right and put her foot down.

'Hey!' Exley glanced across at her. 'Aren't we going the wrong way?'

'For you maybe,' grated Frieda, 'but not for me.'

The Suzuki gathered speed, bouncing up the pathway. 'Wh-what're you doing?' Exley clung on to his seat as the vehicle bucked and swung. 'She's armed, Mrs Cansfield. Armed and insane.'

'Aye,' snapped Frieda, 'and she's got my boy.' She hunched over the wheel, pressing the accelerator to the floor so that the Suzuki hurtled straight at the barn, gathering speed.

'Stop!' croaked Exley. He brandished the shotgun. 'Stop now, or I'll shoot.'

'No you won't.' She didn't even glance at him. 'I'd fasten my seat-belt if I was you.'

Exley watched, horrified, as the barn loomed. When it finally dawned on him what the woman meant to do, he flung the gun away with a yodel of terror and ducked, wrapping his arms round his head. As he did so, Wanda Free ran out of the barn, planted herself in the Suzuki's path and started shooting. As the first bullet hit the windshield, Frieda Cansfield flicked her lights to full beam and drove at the dazzled woman. Wanda squeezed off a couple more shots, trying for the headlamps, then flung herself to one side. The Suzuki hit the barn doing fifty miles an hour. Exley, beltless, was propelled through the shattered windshield on to the vehicle's bonnet, which had smashed through the ancient planking and was now inside the barn. Frieda hit her belt release, kicked open the buckled door and rolled out, keeping her head down. Free, her vision clearing, shot at the woman, but the Suzuki was between them. Cursing, the mad exabiologist started to move round the back of the vehicle, seeking a clear shot. While she was thus engaged, her three young captives emerged and began running towards the goose-house.

Frieda, crouching against the vehicle's battered flank, saw them go and smiled tightly. By getting right down and peering under the Suzuki, she could see Wanda's legs. Keeping one eye on her opponent she worked swiftly, unscrewing the petrol cap, taking matches from her anorak pocket, striking one. Wanda had her in sight and was taking aim when she flicked the lighted match into the Suzuki's tank and flung herself clear.

'Hey, look at that!' Ben, crouching by the goose-house window, pointed. The others looked.

'Mum's car!' cried Barry. 'It's exploded.'

'It's OK,' said Midge. 'She's not in it. I saw her run.'

'Bullet must've hit the tank,' said Ben.

Midge shook her head. 'I don't think so, Ben. I think Mrs Cansfield did it on purpose. She rammed the barn and set fire to the car. She saved our lives.'

'What, my mum?' Barry frowned. 'Don't sound like 'er, that don't.'

'Look!' cried Midge. 'There's Wanda. She's running into the barn.'

'She's crazy,' said Barry. 'That place is bone dry. It'll go up in no time.'

'Trying to save her pets, I bet.' Ben shivered. 'I hope she's too late.'

They stood in the doorway, watching the flames. The fire was spreading fast. One side of the barn was a mass of flame, the Suzuki a skeleton of warped and incandescent metal. Flames leapt into the sky and shoals of sparks whirled away as the roof caught. There was a roaring, crackling noise and they felt the heat on their faces making them move well back. They'll see this in the village, thought Ben. If anyone's awake. He hoped his parents were asleep. His eyes smarted with tiredness and watching the blaze. He realized he didn't care what happened next. His appetite for adventure had evaporated. He wanted to go home.

He was about to mention this to Midge when Dan Cansfield came running from the house, followed by a policeman. There were other figures in the distance, too. Dan was shouting something to the policeman, pointing to the barn, urging him on.

'What's he doing?' gasped Ben. 'That thing's going to collapse any second.'

'It's us!' cried Midge. 'Dan must think we're still in there. Come on.'

They ran towards the two men, calling and waving, but the roar of the blaze drowned their cries. The men had almost reached the barn when something moved in the doorway and Rex Exley tottered out, dragging one leg. He saw the men and waved his arms, shouting. A fragment of what he was saying reached the children. The word *hydrogen*. The policeman shouted something back, and then the three came hurrying towards the goose-house, half carrying Exley whose clothes were smoking.

They were barely halfway when there was a tremendous explosion. The searing blast skittled them, felled the children and shattered the goose-house window. Ben, on his back, saw a gigantic fireball where the barn had been. Bits of burning debris hurtled up and out in every direction, curving down, drawing smoke arches in the dawn sky.

He tried to get up. Nothing hurt, but he couldn't make anything move. Not that it mattered. He smiled. Nothing's falling on me. There are no dragons. No proof. Nobody's waiting for me in the churchyard. Somebody's waiting in the bus shelter. I'm light and happy and here comes the sun with his Mona Lisa smile to shine on my lovely—

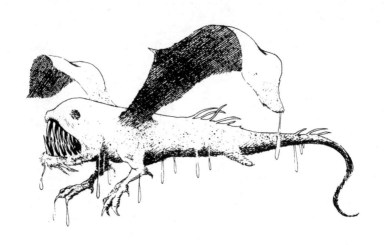

F I F T Y - O N E

—gate. He blinked, looking up. The dawn sky had become a ceiling. It was the ceiling of his room. He recognized the crack, the mark like a laughing face where Dad missed with the emulsion. There was a curtained window where the barn should be and, when he looked for the farmhouse, he saw his mother in the old wicker chair.

She smiled. 'Hello, dear. How are you this morning?'

'I'm OK, I think.' He frowned. 'How did I get home so quick?'

His mother smiled. 'Constable Aspinall drove you in his car.'

Ben shook his head. 'I don't remember. Has he gone now?'

She chuckled. 'He certainly has, Ben. He brought you

home very early on Thursday morning and today's Saturday.'

'Saturday?' He tried to sit up but the bed spun and he fell back, closing his eyes. He felt his mother's hand cool on his forehead. 'Lie still,' she murmured. 'You've been concussed. Dr Thurlow says you're to rest for a day or two.'

Ben smiled wanly. 'But I have, Mum, haven't I? I can't believe it's Saturday.' He remembered something and his eyes flicked open, apprehensive, seeking hers. 'Midge. Is Midge all right?'

'She's fine, Ben. Her mother phoned this morning. Midge is getting up today and she's been asking after you.'

'Has she, Mum? Really?'

His mother smiled. 'Yes, really. I thought that would make you feel better, Ben.'

'Oh, it has.' Ben smiled. He was blushing but he didn't care. 'Can I get up today, Mum? Can I go and see her?'

'Certainly not.' His mother's tone was severe, but she was smiling. 'Midge won't run away, Ben. You can see her tomorrow, if you stay in bed for the rest of today, and if you eat something.'

'OK.' He turned his head on the pillow, looking at her. 'Don't you want to ask me anything, Mum? Like what was I doing up Cansfield at two in the morning?'

His mother nodded. 'Of course I do, Ben, but not just yet. You've had a terrible experience, and your dad and I want to give you a chance to get over it. There'll be plenty of time later for questions.'

It wasn't till his mother had gone that Ben realized he hadn't asked about Barry, or Barry's mum who had saved his life. And what about Wanda Free? Where was she now? And Exley, and old Dan? Did any trace remain of Wanda's pets? Does the world know we were telling the truth – the world and Mrs Tattersall at the *Journal*.

He turned on his side and snuggled down. Warm, safe and sleepy. He smiled. Plenty of time later for questions.

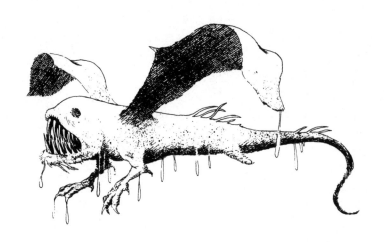

FIFTY-TWO

'Hi, Midge.'

'Hi, Ben.' She shifted along the bench so he could sit beside her. 'How's things?'

'Oh, not bad. You?'

'So-so. Your mum told mine you lost your memory.'

'For a bit, yes. It's OK now.'

'Good.'

'Oh, I got something for you. Here.'

'What is it?'

'The green shades. See – I didn't forget that, did I?'

'You're crazy, Ben. But thanks.'

They watched the traffic build up in the Sunday morning sunshine. After a while, Ben said, 'What've you heard, then? Is Mrs Cansfield all right?'

Midge nodded. 'She lost her eyebrows when the Suzuki went up, but she's a changed woman according to Barry.'

'You've seen Barry?'

'Ah-ha. Yesterday, in Tarkington's. He was with his dad, shopping.'

'Old Dan shopping? You're kidding.'

'No, I'm not. He's gone all quiet, apparently. She tells him to do things and he does them. Barry looked really smug.'

Ben nodded. 'My dad says Wanda Free's vanished. Some guy from NASA came poking around but they haven't found her.'

'No, I know. Barry says she went up with the barn, but Exley told the fuzz she was never in there.'

'Where is Exley?'

'I dunno. He was with the police Friday, but they had to let him go, apparently. Insufficient evidence, Dad says.'

'And what about us? Does everybody still think we were playing games?'

Midge shrugged. 'Hard to tell. The explosion left no trace of the monsters, and of course the Cansfields're keeping mum, but Len Tench found the one we saw, dead and showed it to Major Fairbairn. Len took Ken Aspinall to look at it, but it'd vanished. I don't think Ken believed him, but he had to take the Major seriously. Old Len keeps saying, "I seen what I seen." You know what he's like.'

'So at least one person knows we didn't lie?'

'Oh, several. The Cansfields. Exley. Free, wherever she is. We'll never be able to prove it though, so we'll just have to say what Len Tench says – we seed what we seed.'

'You and me then.' He looked at her sidelong. 'What about us?'

Midge grinned. 'What about us, Ben?'

'Well.' Ben felt his cheeks redden. 'Will we still – you know – see each other? Go round together?'

She mocked him with her eyes. 'Is that what we've been doing, Ben – going round together?'

'I thought it was, Midge, yes.'

She pouted. 'Well, I suppose we might as well carry on then.'

'You won't go off to Scotland or Wales? Your folks haven't got their eye on a nice little restaurant in Timbuctoo?'

She laughed. 'No. They've decided it's bad for me, moving around all the time. Disrupts my education, Mum reckons. So. We'll be staying here, Ben. That's the good news. Do you want the bad news?'

'Hit me with it.'

'No more midnight rendezvous here in the good old shelter.'

'Oh, nuts! Why not?'

'My folks feel they've not been taking sufficient interest in me as a person. This is Dad talking. Since they nearly lost me down the throat of a creature from Jupiter, he's noticed I'm a person.' She chuckled. 'They've hired a chef, so one of them can always be home at night. They mean to keep an eye on me from now on.'

'Oh, Midge! What a drag for you.'

She shook her head. 'You're wrong, Ben. It's not a drag. It's great. I can talk to them now. Tell them things. You know?'

Ben nodded. 'I suppose so.' He looked up as a shadow fell on them. An elderly couple looked into the shelter and, seeing them on the bench, decided to stand outside. Ben smiled. 'It's OK,' he said. 'We were just leaving.'

They walked in the sunshine, holding hands. Ben said, 'I forgot to tell you, Midge. Constable Aspinall's getting a promotion. Sergeant Aspinall. He'll be leaving the village.'

'Good.' Midge smiled. 'He's a nice guy. He deserves it, but who's going to water the bushes behind the shelter?'

'Huh?' Ben looked at her, and saw that smile.

That Mona Lisa smile.

THE END